Time & Space

a short story collection by
Gord Rollo

Also by Gord Rollo

The Jigsaw Man

Strange Magic

Valley of the Scarecrow

The Translators

Crowley's Window

The Dark Side of Heaven

Peeler

Gods & Monsters Vol. 1

Time & Space Vol. 2

Flesh & Blood Vol. 3

Copyright © 2016 by Gord Rollo

Marcela Transmuting © Gord Rollo and Gene O'Neill

Memories of a Haunted Man © Gord Rollo and Everette Bell

All rights reserved. No part of this book may be reproduced or transmitted in any form by any means, electronic or mechanical, including photocopying, recording or by any information storage and retrieval system without permission in writing from the author.

This is a work of fiction. Any resemblance it bears to reality is entirely coincidental.

Published by **Ashbury Creek Media**
Ontario, Canada

Book & Cover Design by **Adam Geen**
www.adamgeen.com

Time & Space

TABLE OF CONTENTS

Introduction	9
Timothy Meek	11
Marcela Transmuting	37
(Co-written with Gene O'Neill)	
All That Glitters…	67
Unnatural Selection	87
The Suicide Man	103
Beneath a Templar Cross	129
Genocide	151
Memories of a Haunted Man	163
(Co-written with Everette Bell)	
Lost in a Field of Paper Flowers	177

INTRODUCTION

Call me insane (*and trust me, many have*) but I happen to love fiction that is set in a different time than present day. Especially dark fiction; obviously. The author can set their stories in the far future or way back in the past — there is just something about different timeframes that turn my crank. Being a fan of that sort of thing, it's natural that I like to dabble in writing futuristic tales and historical horrors too, so for this collection I've tried to gather together some of my personal favorites that deal with this topic.

I've also included some of my best tales that stray a bit closer to Science Fiction and Fantasy than I'm normally known for. I simply love good stories that blur the lines between genre and nothing pleases me more than writing something that the reader is sure fits into one particular genre and then I pull the rug out from underneath their feet at the last minute. To me, fiction should have meaning and the characters should have something to say about life or love or whatever, but I've always subscribed to the notion that fiction should also be fun. Especially short fiction. These shorter length tales are always where I like to let loose and go a little crazy (*crazier???*) which is why I love writing them so much.

Inside *Time & Space* you're going to find stories that deal with horrors from hundreds of years in the past all the way to my futuristic vision of the end of the world. I'll give you some thoughts on evolution and perhaps *de-evolution* as well. We'll talk about painful memories, stress filled deadlines, and how some people try to fool themselves into thinking time can heal all their pain. Here's a spoiler — it can't! We'll also explore inner space, deadly subterranean caverns, and the dark passageways of the comatose human mind. In short, we're going to have some fun.

Lots of it, I hope, so grab a chair, sit back, and try and relax.

Let's spend some quality time together…

TIMOTHY MEEK

Seek ye the Lord, all ye meek of the earth, which have wrought his judgment; seek righteousness, seek meekness: it may be ye shall be hid in the day of the Lord's anger.
-- Zephaniah 2:3 (King James version)

Buffalo, New York, USA
June 14th, 2039

Tim was scared of a lot of things — admittedly, too many damn things — but at the moment his biggest fear was that he'd run out of duct tape before finishing; not that there was much he could do about it. The stores were all closed now, and more than likely sold out or looted long ago anyway. He'd either have enough silver tape to finish sealing the apartment in heavy clear plastic or wouldn't. Simple as that.

Heaven help me if I run out, though, Tim thought. He was getting itchy just thinking about it and needed to stop and go wash his hands again.

Fucking germs...

Tim scrubbed and scrubbed and scrubbed his hands

practically raw, but eventually got himself under control and headed back to work, worried he was taking way too long. There was only the big dining room window left to cover but he knew he was running out of time. Back a few hours ago when he'd taken his last break there had still been four hours to prepare, but time was flying and down to a little over two hours until crunch time now. One way or another, the world as he knew it was about to end. The planet wasn't going anywhere, of course, but human civilization certainly might be. Two hours and change until the scientists and global leaders initiated *Project Red* and finally found out if they could stop the devastation they'd unleashed.

Tim didn't have much faith in them.

None, actually, which is why he was taking his own precautions.

His friends and neighbors here in the building thought he was insane but he'd fully expected that much. The President of the Earth Council himself had ordered (not asked, or suggested, or pleaded — *ordered*) that every able bodied man, woman, and child be outside at 8:00 p.m. Eastern Standard Time tonight for the scheduled bomb drops in his area. *Screw that!* When the sky turned red tonight Tim planned to be in his apartment, cocooned inside his little fortress of plastic. There's just no way he could handle being outside tonight. Not with all the bugs. He was starting to sweat just thinking about them crawling all over his skin…in his ears…in his mouth. *God no!* They'd be too small to see, but still, he wasn't doing it. He *couldn't* do it. Was he making a big mistake, like everyone told him he was? Who knows? They'd all find out soon enough.

From his window, Tim could see people already

starting to gather in LaSalle Park beside his apartment building. He was on the fourth floor and his dining room window looked directly out over the kid's play park and ball diamond beyond it. Downtown was only a few clicks west from here, and Lake Erie directly to the North but distances and directions didn't really mean much in the grand scheme of things anymore. The coming apocalypse had reduced everything down to the here and now. Even though LaSalle Park was fairly small Tim imagined it would hold several thousand bodies if they packed it to the max, but so far there were only a hundred or so men and women milling around, most huddling together with the people they'd arrived with and keeping a close eye on the sky.

Tim was reaching for his last roll of tape, just about to seal the window up when he spotted a familiar face outside in the park. A woman named Wendy Harding was exiting the building and walking into the growing crowd below. All five-feet-eight, blond-haired, long-legged, perfect-bodied inch of her. Even at a time as dire as this, her beauty stopped Tim cold and he let the heavy plastic wrap drop to his feet, forgotten for a moment. Secretly he'd been in love with Wendy for years, and although Tim had promised himself one day he would walk up and let her know how he felt, he'd never summoned up the courage to actually talk to her. The closest he'd ever come was sneaking one of her real estate business cards off the community cork board down in the lobby and dialing her cell phone number listed at the bottom of it. He'd waited until she'd said hello twice, then hung up before making a fool of himself trying to ask her out on a date. He just always figured someday he'd ask her properly, you know…face to face.

Odds were, now he'd never get the chance.

With a sigh of regret, Tim got back to the business at hand and finished sealing off the dining room window. Just to be sure, he took another twenty minutes rechecking every nook and cranny of the seams for possible leaks where the chemicals or man-made viruses or whatever the fuck else might try getting in, but things were about as good as he was going to get them. For better or worse, he was ready.

He needed to go wash his hands again, though.

Fucking viruses...

And then Tim got out his journal.

Project Red Survival Journal
Entry #1
June 14th, 2039

My name is Timothy Meek. I'm 38 years old and I live in apartment 412 of LaSalle Towers, in Buffalo, New York. I'm not very good at describing myself, but I guess I'm about 5' 8"tall and weigh 160 pounds. I'm a pretty average white guy - Caucasian I think they call it — with short brown hair and hazel colored eyes. Suppose none of that really matters all that much but it makes me feel better knowing there will be documentation of me if things go to hell in the coming days, which is definitely possible. There may not be anyone around to read this journal either, but as far as I can see it, it can't hurt.

For the record, I disagree with the Earth Council's desperate decision to implement Project Red, and have subsequently locked and sealed myself within my apartment and will be disregarding the President's order to be outside at 8:00 p.m. tonight. I am not in principle a troublemaker or a lawbreaker, but I have made my decision and must stand by it now. If the truth be told, I hope the government scientists are right but I don't think they will be. If I'm wrong and ever called out to answer for my disobedience, so be it. I'll deal with it then.

I'll try to keep this record simple and to the point as much as possible, even though I'm sure I'll end up rambling. My personal feelings and thoughts aren't all that important so I'll try just relating the facts and the play by play as things go down. No promises though. Okay, in case whoever reads this has no idea what happened, let me go back about six months and tell you what started all this madness.

On January 19th of this year, there was a terrible explosion at one of the United States major centers for disease control in Atlanta, Georgia. Deep within the bowels of the CDC, there was a hidden laboratory where top secret research into biological and chemical weapons had been going on for nearly 100 years. Joe Public like me would never know about any of this but the scientists had really fucked up this time and accidentally released a nasty genetically mutated superbug that swept across the planet killing 60 million people in the first 3 weeks alone. The virus, known only as V-2283 initially (before everyone realized we'd been given a one way ticket to Hell and someone clever in the media had dubbed it Dante's Flu) was an airborne disease that started with flu-like symptoms such as cough and fever but soon escalated to weeping sores, internal hemorrhaging, and liver, kidney, and respiratory failure. Basically, within a week of contact, a person's body would shut down on them, Dante's Flu eating them from the inside out.

The viral weapon had been designed to masquerade as a common cold or mild flu so the infected individual would have time to make it back to their troop, army, country, whatever, and then pass it along before the real symptoms hit. By the time their doctors and leaders discovered what was really happening, it would already be way too late.

Somewhat luckily (if 60 million casualties can ever be considered lucky), the bio-weapon didn't quite work as planned or it might have killed off every man, woman, child, and animal on the planet. When the death rates started to slow down on their own, the Earth Council began to think maybe we'd gotten off as easy as possible under the circumstances, but they were flat out wrong. Those who didn't catch Dante's Flu and die quickly weren't getting away scott free. They weren't immune to the bug as initially hoped; their bodies just reacted differently to the spreading disease. Long story short; the entire world population is dying of cancer.

So am I, I guess.

It's in our lungs, they say. In our blood. I don't seem to have any of the visible lumps most people are developing and I've never even once coughed up a mouthful of blood but I'm sure it's only a matter of time. The government says if we do nothing, we'll all be dead within a year. What we need is a miracle, but what the Council has given us is Project Red. Starting tonight, the bug bombs are going to heal us, supposedly. Well, obviously not me. I'll be sitting this one out.

The clock read 7:52 p.m. and Tim can't recall the city ever being this quiet before. Hell, this was Buffalo after all. Morning until night, this city was *always* crazy. Not tonight, though. Nothing was moving around out there and no one was talking. All those desperate people gathered outside and it was as silent as a tomb. It was seriously creeping Tim out. Through the dining room window he could see a mass of blobs down in the park but the thick plastic was distorting his view and he couldn't make anything out clearly. Probably for the best. If he could see the people outside, his best guess was they'd all be facing the same direction; heads tilted to watch the horizon, waiting to catch their first glimpse of the planes they hoped were coming to save them.

Tim sat down, back against the outside wall and tried to clear that haunting image out of his head but just couldn't shake it. Then he started to imagine the people a few minutes from now, standing out there covered in the bugs raining from the sky and he nearly lost it. Suddenly light headed and nauseous Tim closed his eyes, grabbed his knees and held on tightly.

How can they do it? How can they just stand there and let...

Tim dashed to the sink to vomit.

It was only after washing his face and thoroughly scrubbing his hands again that he realized he hadn't sealed the drain in the kitchen sink yet, like he'd planned. He had lots of bottled water and buckets to use for washing himself or going to the bathroom and had already sealed the bathroom tub and sink, but not this one in the kitchen. *Idiot!* The bombs would be dropping any minute and he clearly wasn't ready. Tim knew the sink had a water trap inside the pipe that would more than likely keep the bugs out but didn't want to take any chances so he quickly twisted in the drain plug, filled the sink with water, layered plastic over the top and used the last of the duct tape to seal the edges to the countertop.

He finished just in time to hear the drone of the approaching plane engines and ran to the dining room window even though he couldn't see outside very well. Seconds later, the blurry crowd below started to cheer and there was even a brief chant of USA...USA... that started up but for the life of him Tim had no idea what they were all so happy about. Desperation and blind faith can do strange things, he guessed.

Fucking people...

Through their collective noise Tim heard the first of

several detonations. Maybe it was because he was sealed inside a plastic bubble, but the bombs sounded strangely muffled and farther away then they really were; more of a bass deep *THUMP* than the loud explosions he'd been expecting. Then again, these weren't missiles smashing into buildings or tearing up the ground; these warheads had been designed to blow up in mid air, to release their payload above the heads of the gratefully cheering crowds.

Tim considered turning on the television set to watch the drama unfolding simultaneously around the globe but his heart just wasn't into seeing the end of the world in blazing Technicolor right now. *No thanks*. He'd eventually want to check the news feeds to get updates on how things were going, but tonight he was far too depressed to watch the idiotic smiling faces of the reporters on CNN. Instead, Tim turned on the portable air compressor and homemade filtration system and said a little prayer they'd hold out long enough for the air outside to clear. It might be a couple of days; it could take as long as a week. Regardless, he was on his own for a while.

Outside, the sky was turning red.

Project Red Survival Journal
Entry #2
June 15th, 2039

Project Red is supposed to purify our blood; hence, in my opinion, the rather silly name. To do that, the scientists have developed these tiny creations called nanobots: microscopic 'bugs' that are half living organism and half computerized machine. Crazy stuff straight out of science fiction novels if you ask me, but they've been around for a while now and will be released into the air by the billions and infected people will breath them into their lungs where they can then apparently go to work healing the sick from the inside out. Call me cynical, but I don't buy it that the scientists have just come up with this wonderful cure. That reeks of bullshit to me. There was too much money in NOT curing cancer, if you know what I mean? Governments keep things from the public all the time and there's no way of knowing when they actually discovered a possible cure. Probably years ago. Decades maybe. It just took the whole world standing at death's door before they finally decided to let the rest of us in on the plan.

How inhaling laboratory created bugs can possibly cure cancer is beyond me, but from what I've gathered they will use electrical impulses to stop the damaged cells from reproducing uncontrollably, not allowing the cancer to grow and spread as it normally would unchecked. It's a bit like chemotherapy, but on a microscopic level where the smart bugs can identify and destroy the cancerous cells on a one on one basis instead of just wiping out everything in its path like chemo. If Project Red works as planned, the world should go into remission, the cancer stopped in its tracks from spreading or infecting other organs. Further nanobots may need to be deployed on a regular basis to keep people's enhanced immune system running properly but no one really knows what the future might bring. At least the smart bugs will give the world a chance, they say.

I'm not buying any of it.

I think it's a crock of shit. A desperate move made by a handful of controlling desperate men and women. Lies and false hopes given to the people to help keep the masses from panicking too much. Hope is a powerful weapon, and as long as the people have some the authorities will be able to keep the peace. Once it's gone, though, and the citizens of the world know they've been played for fools; that's when the shit will really hit the fan. I'm afraid that's where we're headed.

Anarchy.

The next two days were surprisingly uneventful. Tim sat around the dining room table listening to the radio and occasionally flopping on the living room couch to watch an hour or two of the unending television coverage. There was no end to the parade of scientists and government officials interviewed by the various news media; all of which droned on and on about the apparent success of Project Red and how everyone would start feeling better soon. To Tim, it seemed like they were jumping the gun a little, clapping each other on the back a bit too hard before there was any proof they'd accomplished anything. In fact, if success was so assured as they claimed, why weren't they showing more live coverage from out in the cities? Where were the interviews with the average citizens of the world who were supposedly out there on the mend? Sure, there were hours of footage from the night the bombs had been dropped, film clips from around the world of the skies changing color and all the happy people dancing in the streets literally covered head to toe in a sticky red substance that, no matter how many times Tim watched the replays, couldn't stop thinking looked eerily like they were covered in bucket loads of blood.

The following morning, Tim heard a report on the radio that definitive proof had been collected to verify the nanobots were doing their job, stopping the spreading cancer in its tracks. Encouraged, Tim had flipped on CNN to see what they had to say about it, but was shocked to find out all they were showing was a minute long film clip of a bearded man in a white lab coat standing inside some sterile looking lab somewhere.

He was pointing to a graph on a blackboard and explaining about the growing number of reported cases of remission throughout the world. That was it. No patient interviews. No eyewitness reports. No tear-filled mothers or wives beaming at the cameras while they hugged their victorious husband or child who'd just been given a new lease on life. It didn't make any sense, did it? Throughout the day, there were more miraculous newsflashes but they too lacked any real substance. It was all happening too fast for Tim's liking. All the reports were just that little bit off, not quite ringing true or providing any real proof of anything other than the confident scientists claims. And why should Tim believe what they were saying? It was them, along with the governing officials who'd got everyone into this mess in the first place.

Fucking politicians...

Outside his building, Tim couldn't see or hear a thing. After the crowds had dispersed from LaSalle Park swarming with their microscopic saviors several nights back, everything had been quiet as a mouse. No one seemed to be moving around and Tim couldn't even hear the normal yelling and screaming within the paper thin walls of his apartment building. What were they all doing, he wondered? Why was everybody staying inside and being so quiet? Tim had absolutely no idea. All he could go by was what he'd seen and heard on the television and radio — and they weren't telling him shit.

In the days that followed, things would only get worse. Tim continued his journal entries but outside the world had seemingly ground to a halt and there was never much for him to say. The newscasters and scientists were still spouting their messages of hope and victory but even to Tim's untrained eyes he could see the men and women on his television screen didn't appear anywhere near as healthy as their reports claimed. The red lesions and cancerous growths were far more prominent than before, covering huge areas of the broadcaster's visible bodies. These were examples of the scientist's success stories? Christ, they looked worse than before the bombs had been dropped. Worse than Tim, even, and he hadn't showered in over a week now. He quickly stripped and checked again, but Tim still had none of the red growths growing anywhere on his body.

Project Red Survival Journal
Entry #9
June 23rd, 2039

Something has gone terribly wrong. I don't have any proof yet but my gut is telling me things are spinning out of control and the government is lying to the public to try and keep us calm. Was lying, I should say. CNN stopped broadcasting this morning at around 9:30 a.m. and they were the last of the television markets still on the air. Now there is nothing but static and white noise on every station, and the radio signals went dead a few days ago.

The last programming I saw was a badly pieced-together documentary explaining how the bio-engineered nanobots had been created using microscopic computer chips fused with genetic DNA from some small creature. I can't be positive but I don't think they ever revealed exactly which type of bug they took the DNA from. Not that it matters much, I guess, but at the time I remember wondering if the program had been edited and several minutes of information conveniently removed. It didn't make much sense but I had a feeling I was right. Why bother, though? What did they have to hide?

Time & Space

After the documentary, things got even weirder. They cut to a live feed from CNN headquarters in Atlanta, Georgia but there was no one in front of the camera. I kept waiting for the producer to cut to a different feed or run some other pre-taped program but nothing happened. Ten seconds went by, then half a minute. It was as if the studio was empty, or maybe everyone had gone home and just left the camera running. After nearly five minutes of dead air, an old grey haired man with small beady eyes shuffled into view and sat down on the corner of the wooden desk to take center stage in the news studio. He was rake thin and practically drowning in his baggy clothes. His exposed head and hands were also covered in numerous red cancerous growths but he had a constant smile plastered on his face that no amount of sickness seemed able to wipe off. Who was this guy? He had a CNN tag on his chest and although it was a little blurry, when I moved closer to the TV I think his name was Jim something. Jim Argen…something; the last part of the man's name was lost in a fold of his baggy sweater. Whoever he was, surely he wasn't one of CNN's newscasters. Couldn't be. Hell, the old bugger had to be close to eighty years old. Maybe older. He'd walked onstage from behind the angle of the camera though, so for all I knew maybe he was the cameraman; or used to be. Was that even possible, and even if it was why was CNN broadcasting him live to the entire world? I had no way of knowing but I had the feeling that maybe he was the only one left at the studio. Some old diehard who'd worked there his whole life and now, even when the world was falling apart around him, stubbornly refused to go home.

I never did find out. Old Jim just kept sitting there smiling into the camera until the picture cut out and the network went static. After that I had no contact with the outside world at all. No TV, no radio, no noisy neighbors, no nothing.

What the hell is going on?

A couple of days they'd said. Three or four tops. The skies would clear and people could go about their regular lives while the nanobots worked their invisible magic from the inside. Lying bastards. They've fucked things up good this time.

Real good.

When Tim woke up the next morning, naked and sweating beneath an old wool blanket, it took him a moment to figure out there was something different about his surroundings. Something had changed and it wasn't until he got shakily to his feet and walked over to the dining room window that he realized what it was.

Outside, the sky had turned back to blue.

Incredible as it seemed, it was true. Beyond his plastic sheets, the world seemed to be returning to normal. Maybe the scientist had been right after all. Their time frames had been off a week or so, but still, here was finally the potential proof Tim had been waiting for. Trouble was, he couldn't really see out the window to see if things were back the way they used to be or not. The thick layer of plastic obscured everything. He couldn't even tell if anyone was outside in the park.

The urge to tear off the protective sheet was incredible, but Tim stopped himself in time and sat down to think things through first. The last thing he wanted to do was unseal his room too early and contaminate his sanctuary with bugs. In his mind, he could picture millions of microscopic creatures straight out of a science fiction movie hovering outside, just waiting for their chance to get inside and attack him. Even though he was sweating, the thought made him shiver.

Fucking Nanobots...

No way. Opening the window was out of the question.

At least until he had more proof than a blue sky to go on. An idea flashed into his mind about how he used to coat the windows of his old apartment with plastic to keep the cold weather out in the winter. Someone had shown him that if you took a hairdryer and blew warm air onto the plastic, it magically stretched tightly onto the window frame and became almost transparent. The plastic on these windows was much thicker than that old stuff he'd used, but there was a chance it might work the same way. Worth a try, at least.

Hurrying to the bathroom, Tim grabbed his old hairdryer from under the sink and ran an extension cable over to the wall plug on the far side of the room to fire it up. Careful not to put the nozzle too close to the surface in case the hot air melted a hole through the plastic, Tim soon had the window stretched taut on the frame and he could finally see outside again for the first time in ten days.

Outside, Lasalle Park looked pretty much like it always had, except there was still a thin dusting of red powder covering the ground. It looked like someone had snuck into the park and coated all the grass and trees with sticky cotton candy. The sky was incredible though, the most amazing crystal clear cloudless sky Tim could remember and staring at it brought a huge grin to his unshaven face. At least until he realized that there was nothing moving in it. He studied the skies for several minutes but never found a thing. No birds, no bees, no airplanes, no nothing.

Turning his attention back to the ground, Tim was convinced there was nothing going to be visible there, either. On first glance he was right. Where were all the people? Surely if they'd all been cooped up the last week and a half like him, they'd be dying to get out there and move around on such a beautiful day. The kids at least would be out bombing around in the park, right? Apparently not.

Then Tim heard a dog bark below him and it was music to his ears. He leaned forward to press his head close to the glass so he could see straight down closer to the side of his building, eager to see at least some sign of normal life.

That was when he screamed.

Project Red Survival Journal
Entry #10
June 24th, 2039

I woke up in Hell this morning.

That's not me trying to be symbolic or overly dramatic either; I'm being dead serious. Things are worse than I could have ever imagined. Far worse. I don't know exactly what the scientists have done but I think they've destroyed the world and everything in it. The sky had miraculously turned back to blue today and I'd just begun to hope this nightmare was finally over, but then I heard a dog bark and looked out my dining room window for it. I wish I hadn't, for what I saw outside on the red grass was something I can hardly wrap my mind around, much less describe. It had obviously once been a cute, cuddly pet, but where before its body had been covered in soft shaggy fur it now was sealed within a series of red shell-like plates interlocking like medieval armor. Its head and throat were covered in red sores so thick I wondered how it could still see and breathe. Its withered legs were more like burned sticks and instead of running like any normal dog might, the poor animal could no longer carry its own weight and was pushing itself along the ground on the scaly carapace of its bloated belly.

The dog-creature's pathetic barks echoed like gunshots in the early morning silence, and unfortunately I wasn't the only one to hear them. It didn't take long to draw a crowd. I don't know if I even want to try describing to you the scene that unfolded below me in the park after that. Seriously, you're better off not knowing but I think I'd be doing a disservice to whoever eventually reads this if I don't at least try and make you understand how bad things have become.

Hundreds of people from my apartment building, the surrounding neighborhoods, or wherever began to gather in Lasalle Park again. I call them people but that's only because I can't think of any other word to label them. There are no adequate words for what they've become. These people, these things who used to be human beings walked, slithered, and crawled out of their homes on long spindly limbs that stuck out from hard red bodies, bloated like gas-filled balloons similar to that of the deformed dog. Most of their heads had large weeping deformities that encased their entire skulls in smooth red domes that from my vantage point above looked like shiny motorcycle helmets.

For a few minutes they simply congregated, communicating in a series of guttural grunts, strange clicks, and high-pitched hisses. I'd never heard anything like it before but they sounded almost alien in nature, like the gibberish dialogue for some bad science fiction movie. When the poor dog-creature started yelping in misery again, the human-things pounced on it and began tearing into its scaly hide with their elongated teeth and razor sharp claws. The masses made short work of the unfortunate animal but once the smell of death was in the air, the creatures who had recently been my friends and neighbors began to turn on each other, their bloodlust ravenously awakened. The fight was relatively short but incredibly violent and gruesome. From above it seemed like there were no allies or teams; it was every creature for itself, biting and tearing at anything within reach until more than half of the original number of creatures lay

dead or dying, mutilated on the gore-drenched grassy field.
And then the feeding began.
That part I'm not telling you about. No way. Trust me; some things are better left unsaid.

Tim spent the following few days living in fear, terrified one of those creatures had heard his scream and might come looking for him. When none did, he relaxed a little but still stayed away from the windows during the day and was forced to leave the lights off during the night so no one would know where he was hiding.

On day fifteen, the electricity went out anyway so there were no lights to put on, even if he'd wanted to. His air filtration system was shot too but electricity was the least of Tim's problems. He was nearly out of food and worse, he only had half a jug of water left to drink. When that was gone, Tim had no idea what he would do.

He wondered if things were this bad all over the world. They probably were. Had to be, really, if he thought about it logically. The world government had coordinated Project Red around the globe and if the scientists had screwed things up here in America, odds were they'd royally fucked up everywhere, right? Of course they did.

Fucking Scientists…

Then Tim was struck with another thought, one so sobering it literally sent chills down his back and forced him to sit down for fear his legs might give out. *What if I'm the only one left? The only human?* Crazy as the notion was, the more he considered it the less insane it began to sound. *I mean, how many other people out there are so bug phobic they've sealed themselves in plastic?* Good question. Was there anyone out there on the planet as fucked up as him? He had no way of knowing but he seriously doubted it. Even if there were people who hadn't stood outside for the bombs like they'd been told (and surely there were many), unless they'd taken extreme precautions like he had, the microscopic nanobots would surely have found their way into their homes and ultimately, their bodies by now.

Was he the last man on earth? Was he? It says in the bible that the meek will inherit the earth, but Tim had never dreamed it would come down to a singular meek, him, Timothy Meek, the good book had been referring to. This thought made Tim burst out laughing, startlingly loud in his silent apartment, and the fact he didn't care who — or what — might hear him was his first true indication he was losing his mind. He wondered what had taken him so long to finally snap.

Two days later, just as Tim was sitting at the dining room table swallowing his very last gulp of tepid water, he noticed the growth developing on his left forearm. It was red and scaly and hard as rock to the touch. Frantically, Tim jumped to his feet, stripped naked, and checked the rest of his body but there were no other crimson sores to be found.

Not yet.

Tim sat back down at the table and began to cry.

Project Red Survival Journal
Entry #13
July 3, 2039

This will be my final journal entry. I apologize for my last few entries; they were just the scribblings of a bitter, scared man. I'm feeling better today; a little anyway, and I'll try wrapping this up in a way that makes more sense. I can't go on any longer. Living, I mean. My food and water are gone and worst of all I have many more large red welts developing on my skin. My left hand is already hooked and withered and basically useless to me trapped within its rigid shell. My writing hand, my right, isn't much better and I steadfastly refuse to go look in the mirror to see what has become of my face.

I thought I had the room sealed, I really did, but I suppose I've been kidding myself all along. Really, what was I thinking? There's just no way to completely seal a room air tight enough to keep the nanobots out, not when all you have to work with is heavy plastic and a few rolls of duct tape. It was predictable right from the start that I'd be contaminated along with everyone else; I just managed to prolong things, I guess.

For the record, I'm not angry at anyone and I don't blame the President of the World Council. Hell, he was just doing what he thought best. At least he, along with the rest of the council tried to save everyone and for that I am somewhat grateful. Doesn't mean I'm not pissed off, but what can I do but accept things as they are? I have no idea what will become of the world or the new breed of human creatures that we are all becoming. If they have the capacity, maybe it will be one of them who finally ends up reading my account here on these pages. Who knows? All I am certain of is I have no desire to become one of them. I can't stomach the thought of that. My body is metamorphosing at an incredible rate, the nanobots continuing to work their secret dark magic inside me as I write these last few lines, but while I'm still in control of my body and mind I've chosen to stop this nightmare before it reaches its inevitable conclusion. I know suicide is a coward's way out, but I'm okay with that. Death is the only choice I have.

I won't…I mean I can't…become one of them.

Tim finished writing and closed up his journal. In his heart he knew it was a sadly inadequate collection of entries and didn't come close to explaining the horror of what had happened outside of his walls but he'd done his best to try and make some future inhabitants of earth understand what had become of the human race. Tim sealed the book inside two zip-lock freezer bags and left the journal sitting in the center of the dining room table.

Standing on spindly red legs, he lurched his way over to the kitchen countertop and dug through a drawer of junk until he found what he was looking for: A real estate business card with a picture on it of a pretty blonde-haired women smiling up at him. Moving to the phone, Tim carefully punched in the phone number printed on the woman's card and hoped she'd not only be home, but still be capable of picking up the receiver. Someone answered on the fourth ring, or at least knocked the handset off onto the floor. Tim could hear a series of wet clicking noises, and the sound of heavy, labored breathing.

"Wendy?" Tim asked, knowing she couldn't answer him but refusing to die without at least trying to finally speak to the woman he'd fallen in love with from afar. This might not be the Wendy Harding he remembered and had desired all these years but Tim hoped there was enough humanity left in her she might somehow still understand his words. "It's Timothy Meek from upstairs in apartment 412. I've never had the courage to tell you this but I've always thought you were the prettiest woman I've ever met. I know things are all screwed up now, but I was just wondering if there was anyway you'd consider coming upstairs to meet me. I don't know why, but I think I'd like that a lot. What do you think?"

There was no response. Just more heavy breathing.

"Apartment 412, okay? Come up and say hi, Wendy. Please…"

Tim hung up the phone and went directly into the living room to start tearing off the semi-transparent sheets that had been all he'd seen of the world for so long. Within minutes he'd removed all his hard work and was just rolling the plastic into a big ball when suddenly there was a loud knock at the apartment door. The pounding, which was more of a *thud-scrape-thud* than a real knock, startled Tim but didn't surprise him. Steeling his nerves, not knowing what he'd find but knowing this was how his life would end, Tim took a deep breath and opened up the door.

Outside the door, a massive five-foot-eight red bug stood looking in at him. This was the first time Tim had seen one of the creatures up close and it was only now he noticed the tiny flickering antennae on top of its head and realized what animal DNA the scientists had used to graft onto the nanobots. Unbelievable, but it all made perfect sense really. Everyone had always said they'd be the last creatures alive if the world was stupid enough to engage in Nuclear War. We'd escaped that particular end of days scenario, but somehow, through no real action of their own, these creatures had still managed to come out on top of the food chain after all.

Plain and simple: They were survivors.

The thing that had once been Wendy Harding shuffled into the room with teeth and claws ready, and as hideously deformed as she was Tim still found himself strangely attracted to her. Maybe it was the growing creature within him, or maybe he'd just finally gone completely crazy. Instead of running away or trying to protect himself Tim simply opened his arms and waited for her deadly embrace.

Fucking cockroaches…

Story Notes

I think we all have an idea or at least a best guess as to how the world as we know it might come to an end. Being a horror writer I happen to have many of those scenarios bouncing around in my skull and Timothy Meek is merely one of those possible endings. It's a good one, though; one that doesn't seem all that far-fetched to me if you think about the way diseases and germs can spread and everyone is so scared of the next SARS and Bird or Swine Flu to come along. It wouldn't shock me at all to see some airborne bug mutate into existence or a deadly virus be released out of some government laboratory. I'm actually surprised it hasn't happened yet, to be honest. Time will tell, I suppose.

Anyway, the genesis of this particular story was when I was listening to some Rush cd's and thinking about the end of the world. At the end of the first song on their classic 2112 album the only lyrics on the track are…"And the meek shall inherit the earth." Great tune and great album but it got me thinking. I was wondering if the meek really might inherit the world someday? Doubt it, but it could happen I suppose. And then I thought, well, what if it wasn't all of the meek but maybe just one of them…Timothy Meek, to be exact. Maybe it will be just him who ends up inheriting the world as the last human left standing. Sure…why not? The plot of my story flowed naturally from there…

Marcela Transmuting

"Anger is a great force. If you control it, it can be transmuted into a power which can move the whole world."
--William Shenstone

"Sweet is revenge--especially to women."
--Francis Bacon

Marcela jogged along the Westside biking trail in the park, initially wishing Peter was with her. But he was packing his things at the apartment, their relationship over. She'd come back home unexpectedly early this afternoon and found Peter in their bed with another woman. She had no idea who the petite blonde was, but it didn't matter. Bottom line was Marcela would be living alone now for the first time in seven years, since leaving her native Dominican Republic to attend school here in the City of Angels.

Marcela scoffed at the ridiculous nickname. Peter certainly hadn't turned out to be an angel; that was for sure. Far from it!

Even though Marcela didn't like to run by herself at

night, she'd hoped it would be cooler this late, and she couldn't really stand the sight of Peter. Besides, she asked herself with a flippant sense she didn't really feel, what self-respecting low-life would be out here, now, in this absolutely sweltering sauna? Being from the Caribbean, heat never really bothered her, but she hated the humidity and stifling smog LA afternoons were famous for. And it was indeed muggy, regardless of the late hour: her light green tank top and shorts were soaked with perspiration already, and she hadn't run a quarter mile yet.

Marcela sighed, speeding up slightly.

She didn't need a man in her life right now, anyway. Not with the demands at the office--she was very close to being offered an associate position. She smiled wryly, thinking that maybe this would work out better for her, after all. She'd have more time to do work at home, instead of sitting around fretting about Peter, when he was out supposedly playing three-on-three basketball but actually seeing a girlfriend. In any event, she was resigned to the decision. And really, the idea of being alone didn't seem quite so frightening, now; Sandy was next door, if she needed company.

Maybe, I'm going through some kind of transformation here, Marcela told herself, wiping a wrist sweatband across her forehead. Yeah, finally growing up.

It seemed to suddenly grow darker as the trail curved away from 10th Avenue into the heart of the park. Scary--

That's when she saw them ahead standing in the path, instantly realizing they were wrong, all three wearing black windbreakers in the muggy heat.

Marcela slowed to a walk, eyeing them warily.

As she got closer the three black teenage boys aggressively maintained their position, actually blocking her way on the bike path. Now she could see the funny caricature of a grinning skull on the breast of their jackets, and they were all wearing black satin bandannas on their heads, like defensive backs in the NFL. But she didn't think these boys were playing a game. No indeed.

She came to a halt about ten feet from the three young men, reaching up and nervously stroking her good luck charm hanging around her neck: the tiny silver ball pendant, a smooth and shiny sphere with a hole drilled through the middle.

Well, Marcela thought with forced confidence, maybe those two nights a week studying karate at The Divine Wind will pay off, now. She hoped it wouldn't come to that though. "Can I pass, please?" she asked, with fake bravado, trying to keep her voice from breaking.

"No, momma," the biggest boy said, with a kind of half apologetic tone, shaking his head. "Go 'head, tell her why, Silk."

The smallest boy took a step forward, holding out his hand. "We collectin' toll," he said, an evil smirk on his face.

The big guy nodded at Marcela. "Tha's right, momma. Hope ya'll holdin' somepin' in tha' little purse." He pointed with his left hand at the blue waist purse that contained her apartment keys, a few dollars, and some change, his right hand unbuttoning his windbreaker, revealing a pistol stuffed in the front of his pants.

Oh, my God, she thought, her heart hammering her ribs as the grim reality of the situation began to fully register.

I'm going to be robbed!

The three of them edged closer.

It's now or never, Marcela decided, trying to stave off her growing panic as she lashed out with a front kick, catching the leader a glancing blow with her foot in his upper thigh. She had intended to kick him in the crotch, but she was a trifle off because of her fear, and he was surprisingly quick for his size. He recovered easily, and before Marcela could cover up, he moved in a step or two and lashed out with a punch, smashing her squarely in the face.

Pinwheels of light went off in her head accompanied by sharp, shooting pains. From flat on her back Marcela groaned, fighting nausea, arms protecting her face, immediately knowing that her nose was broken.

Then, they were all over her, and she felt her purse being snatched from her waist...And even worse, hands were pulling down her shorts. She tried to scream once, but she was kicked in the side and pain exploded along her ribcage, fireworks again bursting in her head; and the cry for help stuck in her throat. She felt one of them on top of her, ripping off her tank top, hands roughly clutching her breasts--

Thankful blackness engulfed her as Marcela lost consciousness.

***

She was roused to partial awareness by something... an unusual but strangely familiar sound? Marcela was naked and lying on her side, curled up in a protective ball, hurting all over, one hand squeezed into a tight fist. She managed to lift her head slightly, blinking; but it was much too dark to see anything. She cocked her head, listening.

It was the steady background noise that had roused her--a constant monotonous drone. And the smothering smell of decay. All so familiar. And for a moment, despite the pain, she was flash-backed to last summer, the trip to Costa Rica with Peter, and hiking in the rain forest--the muggy nights in the Central American jungle and the constant background *hum* of a thousand or more insects.

Then she opened her clenched hand; she held the silver sphere they'd bought from a street vendor in San Jose, a spooky old lady with piercing black eyes. Marcela had apparently ripped the charm free of the necklace during the attack, hid it in her hand. She curled her fingers again around the pendant, remembering the old lady had claimed it contained magical protective and restorative powers.

Strange, but as she held the tiny metal ball, it seemed to move within her tight grasp, to expand and contract, pulsing ever so gently. It didn't seem quite as round and smooth, either, her fingers seeking out and finding several small bumps and dents in its previously unblemished exterior.

She tried to move, tried to sit up to take a look but a sharp pain in her side overwhelmed her semi-conscious state, and she sank back down into the relief of cool blackness.

***

The darkness is good. It cools her naked skin and heightens her senses. She is hungry, thirsty too, but she waits patiently for the last few orange rays of light to disappear from the western sky before moving. Wait for it... almost gone... now!

She uncoils her muscular body, running at first for no other reason that to feel the power, experience the rush, relish the surge of adrenaline coursing through her veins as she shoots off into the thick green foliage of the rainforest.
Running, running, running…
Searching…

***

Three days later Marcela was released from the hospital after treatment for shock, a concussion, a broken nose, and two fractured ribs. The three days of lying on her back left her with little to do except think. By the time Peter picked her up in his black BMW and drove her back to the apartment, Marcela had experienced a major attitude change. The idea of living alone, of being a completely independent person, that she'd speculated on just before the rape, was now an accepted fact in her mind.

In the apartment, Marcela curled her feet under her on the couch and listened to Peter fumble. Of course he felt guilty, blamed himself for letting her run alone that night, which was ridiculous.

"I guess, I, ah, should unpack, you know," he said, looking around kind of sheepishly at the cardboard boxes stacked in the front room, containing his tapes and books and sports memorabilia. He nodded to himself, as if agreeing. "I can probably get my deposit on the new place back if I explain--"

"Why do that, Peter?" Marcela interrupted, feeling a little impatient with the whole thing. Absently, her fingers played with the silver ball pendant, the bumps and dents that had marred its surface surely the result of her shocked mind playing tricks on her, because her fingers felt nothing but smoothness now. "You're not staying, you know."

"B-but I thought that…Well, you know," he said, looking confused. "I just thought you'd want me to stay, at least for a little while. The doctors said--"

She forced a smile and shook her head. "That's not necessary. I'll be fine here by myself. Don't worry about it."

"But, you'll be all alone."

She nodded. "I know." Her smile was sincere, now. "I've come to a remarkable realization, Peter: Alone isn't the same thing as lonely. Besides, Sandy is just across the hall."

"Yeah, but after what happened…" Peter looked embarrassed now. Although he'd visited her each day in the hospital, they'd never specifically discussed the rape, her feelings, his reactions in any detail. It was something she'd allowed him to avoid. "For christsakes, Mar, the doctor said it might take months for you to get over the fear, the anxiety attacks, the nightmares and you know, you heard him. Some women need extensive counseling, for years even."

She knew all that.

But even that first night in the hospital, Marcela hadn't been afraid. Maybe it was her Caribbean resiliency, the potent drugs or her Costa Rican pendant that she wore again on a new chain--probably a combination. She'd had a strange dream about running naked through a rainforest, but awakened little more than slightly unsettled--not what she'd call overwhelmed with anxiety. In a way the rape seemed to have accelerated her attitude change. She wasn't afraid or anxious, now, at the prospect of being completely on her own. She'd developed a kind of positive strength during the three days of contemplation in the hospital. She couldn't really explain it. It was just a fact. And it wasn't only about excluding Peter from her life, either. She didn't even want a female roommate, although Sandy had volunteered to move in for a while. No, she had decided, she actually preferred being alone, and though she might be a little apprehensive at times, she knew that, for whatever reason, at least for now, she had become a solitary person. A completely independent being.

They argued for a few more minutes…

But Peter finally agreed that they would separate as planned, before the incident in the park.

Actually, Marcela thought, he'd probably put up only token resistance because he still felt guilty about letting her run alone that night. And the thought made her angry--an uncharacteristic response. Who the hell did he think he was, deciding anything about what she did?

When the final decision was actually spoken out loud and agreed upon, she could read the relief in Peter's eyes. It was time to go their separate ways. And for Marcela, that meant by herself.

"Here," he said, writing down something on a slip of paper beside the phone. "This is my new phone number. If you need me anytime, Mar, just call. Even, if it's the middle of the night. You know, if you have a nightmare or something."

She nodded, agreeing, humoring him. Anything to get him on his way.

At last, Marcela said goodbye to Peter, and sighed deeply with relief when he was finally out the door.

***

The compelling need for solitude extended to everything, including her work. After settling in alone at her apartment that first day, Marcela had called the senior partner in the firm, Ronald Benoit, getting him at two o'clock just as he returned from lunch; and after describing her injuries, she explained that she needed more time off.

"…That's right, Ron."

There was a brief pause. "Well, of course, Marcela, take enough time to gather yourself. I understand. Why don't you call back in a…oh, a month."

Marcela smiled to herself. She knew that Ron was surprised by the request, because the expected thing, the company thing, would be to come right back to work after a day or two. *Best to get right back on the horse*, as the associates would say. Forget the unpleasantness. The macho thing. Of course all the associates were male, and as far as she knew none of them had ever been mugged, raped, or beaten. But, with the present state of her mind, Marcela didn't really care what Ronald Benoit or any of the associates thought.

"I knew you'd understand, Ron," she said, in her sweetest voice, and added silently, *you insensitive bastard.* "Who knows, I might even take a little trip, get away from this heat wave."

"Now, that sounds good," the senior partner agreed. "You do that. And take care. Just give me a call when you're ready to come back."

"Bye, Ron," she said, hoping she screened the finality of tone. Right now Marcela didn't care about the firm at all. She felt like she would probably never go back. And it was an uplifting feeling, bringing her a sense of freedom. *But who knows what I'll feel a month from now?* She advised herself sagely, settling the phone in the receiver, justifying the hedging call to the boss. Maybe she *should* take a trip. Might not be a bad idea, the perfect way to put her troubled and unhappy past life behind her once and for all and make a fresh start.

A new beginning sounded wonderful, but at the moment all she cared about was getting some much needed sleep. Marcela's 24-hour cycle had suddenly changed in the hospital. She wanted to sleep through the day, only feeling alert after dark. Strange, she'd thought, when she'd recognized the sleep cycle shift was permanent, even after leaving the hospital. Perhaps it's all a part of some kind of mystical transformation, along with the attitude change, she told herself, half-jokingly, as she climbed into bed.

***

Running... her sleek body a blur in the night as she sprints toward an unusually strong scent that is tantalizing her senses. She follows it, head moving back and forth, sniffing constantly, the slight breeze blowing inland from the ocean guiding her closer and closer, urging her onward. She's not sure what it is yet, or where it's coming from, but her nipples harden and her mouth starts to salivate, anticipating the inevitable encounter.

Breaking through a row of low bushes, knowing she's getting close now but she pulls up short, skidding to a complete stop, startled to see a black woman standing directly in her path. She recognizes her immediately, as the local Costa Rican woman who sold her the silver ball pendant. The large woman is dressed in layers of sheet, a rainbow of bright colors wrapped around her considerable girth. Her gray hair is braided in many rows using hundreds of hand carved beads.

The black woman raises her hands and smiles. "Peace, my child. Relax and come to me. Come to Semma."

And then the strange woman is gone: a silent explosion of swirling light sucked up and swallowed by the canopy of moisture-swollen clouds handing in the dark sky above.

***

After four days and nights in the apartment, Marcela realized she was feeling bored, restless. The vivid dreams that she'd been experiencing since her rape kept recurring: She was always moving quickly through the Costa Rican rainforest, searching for something. She was searching alone, a solitary hunter. Moving quickly through the undergrowth, looking, looking…but she would always awaken just before she discovered what it was she was searching for. After waking, the mystery disturbed her otherwise tranquil sleep.

Though she never reappeared in her dreams, Marcela found her thoughts returning again and again to the strange woman who'd sold her the silver pendant.

Peace, my child. Relax and come to me. Come to Semma.

Semma? Was that the name of a village in Costa Rica? The woman's name? Marcela had no way of knowing, nor should she care, but she couldn't seem to shake the woman's image or her soothing words from her head.

Come to me.

Without pausing long enough to let the rational side of her personality talk her out of what was surely a crazy, impulsive idea, Marcela found herself on the phone, credit card in hand, booking herself on the next available flight to San Jose, the vibrant and beautiful capital city of Costa Rica. Not sure if she was about to do something stupid or not, she fiddled nervously with the silver pendant around her neck. The perfectly round ball felt remarkably warm to the touch.

***

The Republic of Costa Rica was a small yet glorious place: a diverse, thriving country that had tropical beaches, eco-rainforests, and rugged mountain ranges in equal measure. In the center of this paradise, nestled between two of the higher mountain ranges and therefore protected from the balmy Caribbean and the often merciless Pacific winds, lay a postcard perfect valley, the Meseta Central, where two-thirds of Costa Rica's population lived. San Jose, the vibrant capital city, was home to 300,000 friendly, hard working people. Most were urban dwellers, passionately in love with their city. They wore stylish clothes, were hip to all the latest fashion trends and proudly referred to themselves as *Ticos*. Most lived and worked inside the city limits, happy to leave the fishing industry, or the growing Coffee, Sugar, Banana, or Pineapple plantations to the country farmers. Ticos or farmers, Marcela wasn't here to meet any of them. She was only here to find one person.

And she worked for herself selling trinkets and necklaces to the tourists.

Marcela wasn't at all sure she would be able to track down the strange woman of her dreams in this busy, often chaotic city, but some awakening voice inside of her was adamant that she try. Spanish being her native tongue, Marcela had little difficulty communicating, although even within this small nation there were numerous different dialects spoken, some similar, some vastly different from the language she had grown up speaking in Santo Domingo.

Just steps outside of Juan Santamaría International Airport--located ten miles outside of the city--Marcela hopped on a bus and was soon standing in downtown San Jose. It was mid-afternoon and the city was alive and kicking: people scurrying everywhere, cars and buses honking and jostling for position, and street vendors on bicycles selling fruits and cold beverages out of wicker basket on wheels pulled behind them. It was far busier than Marcela remembered from her last trip here, but at least it would be easy to find someone to help her find the woman she was searching for. As it turned out, she didn't even have to move. A man selling lottery tickets spotted her and rushed to her side before any of his competition beat him to the punch. He was tall, rake thin, very dark skinned and wearing a comically large hat woven from palm leaves that served the duel purpose of shading his bald head from the sun and also attracting customers. He had bad teeth but his smile was genuine so Marcela purchased two tickets and let him keep the change.

"Quizás puede usted ayuda mí, Señor? Trato de localizar alguien," she asked. *Perhaps you can help me, Sir? I'm trying to locate someone.*

The street vendor was more than happy to help, if he could. Marcela told him how she'd been to San Jose last summer with a friend and how she'd purchased a necklace from a large black woman at the nearby local market. The tall man chuckled, explaining how there were a great many large black woman in Costa Rica, and that Marcela would have to give him more information than that.

"Dio se ella su nombre?" he asked.

Her name? Marcela thought. She was just about to say no, she hadn't said her name, but then decided to stretch the truth a little bit and try the name she'd been given in her dream. "Ella me dijo para venir a Semma."

The smile vanished from the tall man's face.

"Dijo usted, Semma?" he asked, his voice rising sharply on the last word as he quickly made the sign of the cross in the air between them.

Marcela nodded, more than a little taken aback at the reaction the man had shown to that name. "Qué es la cuestión?"

What's the matter? she asked, but the man had heard enough. He told her to go away and leave him alone, packing up his tickets and walking away as fast as he could. He seemed genuinely spooked and in a hurry to bolt away from her. He started to do just that, running across the street before turning back to shout something over his shoulder.

"Salga de nuestra ciudad fina. Si es la bruja de vodú que usted busca, usted la encontrará en Puntarenas, pero no dirá yo no lo advertí!"

He ran off without another glance back, leaving Marcela stunned. He'd told her to get out of their fine city and also that she'd find Semma in Puntarenas, a nearby city. Other than the insult to leave, it was actually quite helpful information, but none of that was what stunned her so badly. It was when he'd said, bruja de vodú.

Voodoo witch.

***

The trip to Puntarenas was relatively uneventful. The bus was fairly new, more comfortable that Marcela had expected, and she thankfully had the back seat all to herself. Puntarenas City was only an hour and a half ride from San Jose, a coastal resort used more by locals than by the tourists. Marcela hadn't been there on her last visit and was looking forward to seeing the ocean. She passed the time taking in the scenery and being amazed that the locals actually used machetes to trim the weeds and high grass alongside the roads. Someone could make a fortune if they opened a weed-eater company around here, she thought, smiling.

She stepped off the bus as the sun was setting over Port Caldera, just north of the city, the country's most important port for importing and exporting goods. She had a magnificent view of the ocean and she stood still for several minutes just taking it all in. She was supposedly on vacation, after all. That's what she told herself, anyway. In reality, she was stalling, a little afraid to speak to anyone here since the incident with the lottery ticket vendor back at the airport. Not that she had any choice--Marcela knew she had to ask for help again. She didn't know what she was getting herself into, but she was determined to see this out. As luck would have it, an elderly woman was sitting on a wobbly wooden bench at the entrance to the bus terminal. It didn't appear as if she was waiting for a bus--just resting her weary bones for a while.

Marcela gathered her courage and walked up to the

old woman to ask her if she knew where to find Semma.

"Semma? El templo?" the woman responded.

The Temple? Is that what Semma was? The name of a voodoo temple? Marcela only nodded, not trusting herself to speak. The aged woman looked her up and down for a long time then simply pointed with a shaky, crooked finger in the direction of a dirt road leading away from the city and the ocean. Marcela couldn't see any buildings along the path--not within eyesight anyway--just some scattered palm and banana trees lining the road. Marcela thanked the old woman and was quickly on her way.

She walked for half an hour and found the temple just as the last rays of light were disappearing over the horizon. Semma, if that was indeed the name of this place, was nothing more than a small wooden cottage with a garden full of fruit trees. The only way she could tell this house was different from several other small homes she'd passed was the large elaborate altar sitting on the front porch, and the strong scent of incense wafting out from the suspiciously wide-open front door.

Was this where she'd find the large black woman who'd sold her the pendant, or was she just playing a fools game, dashing off to a foreign land on the strength of nothing more than a dream. Marcela reached up to stroke the silver ball around her neck, taking comfort from its warmth that she was doing the right thing in coming here. She took a deep breath and headed for the porch. A shadow was waiting there to greet her. A large shadow, but it wasn't the person she expected.

A young black man, maybe twenty-two years old, tall and broad shouldered, stood in the doorway waiting patiently for her.

"Welcome to Semma, our Temple," the young man said. "You're too late. My mother, Mambo Ranice has passed."

"You…you speak English," Marcela managed to speak, too shocked at the news of the dream woman's death to say anything else.

"Of course. She taught me many languages, many things. My name is Miguel. She told me to wait here for you. Come. I'll take you to her."

"Take me to her?" Marcela was confused. "I thought you said she—"

But the young man was gone, disappeared into the temple.

"How did she know I was coming?" Marcela asked the empty doorway. Raising her voice, she tried, "Miguel? How do you know who I am?"

No answer, just receding footsteps.

***

Marcela knew that Mambo was the term used for a Voodoo High Priestess and as she followed the mysterious woman's son inside the temple, all she could picture was the tall ticket vendor in San Jose making the sign of the cross in the air at the mention of this place. She wondered if she was making a dreadful mistake, but that tiny voice inside of her was urging her onward, a quiet strength flowing into her body even though she'd been traveling all day and should have been exhausted.

Marcela had never stepped foot inside a voodoo temple before, and it was nothing like what she had expected. It was just a comfortable little house but the main room was adorned with colorful curtains and hanging flags that draped all the way to the spotlessly clean wooden floor. Around the room were several different altars, all with incense burning and various eclectic items on them. Marcela noticed photographs of native people, a small stuffed teddy bear with a pink ribbon, a dinner plate loaded with a collection of smooth stones, tree twigs tied together with a thin leather strap, stamps resting on a letter, yellowed with age, and much more. What she didn't see was blood stained sacrificial knives, terrified animals tightly bound to wooden posts, mindless walking zombies wandering around in search of flesh, or any of the other silly Hollywood images that she's always associated with the Voodoo religion. There *was* an 18 inch indigo lizard stretched out on the room's only sofa, but it was half asleep and seemed friendly enough so Marcela didn't let it bother her. She breathed a sigh of relief and let herself relax. It was easier than she thought it might be. Crazy, perhaps, but here in this strange little temple Marcela soon felt totally at peace--at home.

Miguel wasted no time, getting right down to business. He marched over to a doorway, pausing halfway through a set of curtains made from string after string of red beads. "Follow me, she's in here."

Marcela stepped through the beaded curtain, half expecting someone to jump out and yell *surprise* at any moment, let her in on the game they'd been playing but the young man had spoken the truth--the large black woman who'd sold her the silver ball pendant a year ago, Mambo Ranice, was lying in bed covered in blankets, dead to the world. Her hands were folded respectfully across her chest, and the sheets had become a simple altar, covered in flowers, a few small pictures, and some of the necklaces she'd made. She looked happy, content.

"I'll try and come back to check on you in the morning," Miguel said, bowing slightly, starting to back out of the room.

"What's that supposed to mean?" Marcela briefly panicked, but her inner voice spoke up again and she was sure she knew the answer before the young man replied.

"Lay down. Rest. My mother wishes to speak to you."

With that, Miguel left the room, leaving Marcela with a dead woman she barely knew. Lay down? Rest? Surely he was kidding. There was no way--

But before Marcela could object, she yawned, suddenly fighting to keep her eyes open. She didn't panic. In fact, an overwhelming feeling of calmness washed over her, soothing her doubting mind and letting her see she had nothing to fear in this place of death. The voice within her told her to trust her instincts. She lay down beside the voodoo priestess, and within seconds, was fast asleep.

***

Running...running...

Searching in the dark, sniffing the air, knowing she is getting close.

Her nostrils flare, a new smell replacing, overpowering the old scent. She bursts through the tree line, comes upon a small house, recognizing the temple, recognizing the burning incense, recognizing the lizard...and recognizing the large black woman standing on the front porch. These sights trigger an avalanche of memories and she momentarily forgets about the hunt. Memories breed awareness, and she remembers not only where she is and who stands before her, but also who she is and why she's here.

Mambo Ranice looks exactly as Marcela remembers her: wrapped in layers of bright colorful sheets, her hair braided with small beads. She is smiling and holding her arms out in greeting.

"Be at peace, child. Stay with me awhile."

"But you're dead, aren't you?"

"Maybe, maybe not. On sacred ground, it really doesn't matter. That's why I needed you to come here. I couldn't stay long enough, me coming to you."

"What do you want from me?"

"Nothing, child. Just to talk, to explain what's happening to you. I know you feel the coming change, but you don't need to fear it. Your protector comes."

"I, I don't understand?"

"You don't need to. You just need to believe. There's a power within you, child. I don't know what it is, but I felt it the moment I met you last summer. Your Anifantia spoke to my soul that day, asked me--"

"My what?"

"Your Anifantia. It's your animal within, your spirit guide and protector. It lies dormant within most humans, but yours wants to be set free. That's why I sold you that necklace."

Marcela reaches up and strokes the silver pendant. The bumps and dents have returned. Instead of a perfectly round ball, it has flattened out, sprouting several short appendages.

"What's happening to it?"

"It's becoming, child. Just like you...Just like you...like you..."

Mambo Ranice is starting to fade away, the smoke from the incense starting to seep through her insubstantial form.

"Wait!" Marcela shouts. "Don't leave yet, I still don't understand. This is all crazy talk, isn't it? I mean, really, it's just a dream!"

Mambo Ranice smiles.
"Is it, child? Are you sure?"

***

After returning from Costa Rica, Marcela spent days trying to get her head around everything she'd seen and heard. She still wasn't sure what exactly had happened at Semma, the voodoo temple. When she'd woken up the next morning, she'd found herself all alone in bed. Mambo Ranice's body was gone. Either Miguel had returned in the middle of the night to carry her away, or she had never been there in the first place. Perhaps the heavy incense in the air had been a drug of some sort and she'd inhaled enough of it to cause her to hallucinate. Or maybe she was just going crazy. There was always that possibility. Then again, when she'd checked her silver pendant that morning, it hadn't seemed as round and unblemished as she remembered. It wasn't flattened out, like in the dream, but something about it sure looked--and felt--different. Deep down, she wanted to believe that everything that had happened had been real.

One thing Marcela couldn't deny; she was beginning to change, inside and out. Just as Mambo Ranice had said she would. *The coming change* she'd called it.

That weekend, returning from the corner 7-Eleven store with a bag of essentials--she went out only at night now--her body definitely felt different, not clumsy and sore as one might expect, still recovering from all the recent injuries, but actually strong and powerful. After putting the groceries away, she stripped down and stood naked in front of her dressing mirror, carefully examining herself. Her skin was kind of mottled. She had always been dark, tanning very easily, but now, her body was splotchy. But that wasn't the strangest thing. No indeed. She smoothed both hands along the sides of her breasts.

They were shrinking!

At first, she'd thought it was her imagination. But now she was sure. Her breasts were growing smaller. She turned and looked over her shoulder, her entire figure seemed to be growing boyish--her hips for sure were losing the feminine roundness.

Strange.

Staring at herself in the mirror, Marcela thought, I'm losing my old identity, but growing stronger, feeling more powerful even.

"Jesus, maybe I'm becoming a male," she said aloud and laughed. Dismissing the ridiculous speculation, she whispered, "But what's really happening to me? Is it all in my mind? Actually, the body changes aren't really that pronounced. Maybe--"

There was a rap at the door.

"Hey, Marcela, it's me, Sandy," the familiar voice called through the door. "You know, that weird lady across the hall, the one you seem to be avoiding like a STD. Saw you coming back with groceries. Open up."

Pulling on a kimono-like bathrobe to cover the suspected body changes, Marcela went to the door, paused a moment, then opened it. "Hi, Sandy," she said, forcing a smile.

"Hello, stranger," the thin brunette said, smiling back. "You okay?" There was a puzzled, almost hurt, expression on Sandy's face.

Marcela nodded, then explained, "My trip took a lot

out of me. And actually, been having a lot of cramps since I got back, you know, that time." She shrugged. Of course it was a lie. She hadn't had a period since a month before the attack. And even though she got no more exercise than the occasional nightly walk to the corner store and prowling the apartment, Marcela felt in top health. Oh, she hadn't been eating much, her normally vegetarian diet seeming kind of bland and unfulfilling.

"I understand," Sandy said. "You probably aren't interested in a movie after dinner, are you?"

Marcela smiled and shook her head. The mention of dinner made her aware of a smell, a wonderful smell. She poked her head out in the corridor, noticing that her friend had left her door ajar. The smell was coming from inside Sandy's apartment. "*Mmmm*, what are you cooking for dinner? Smells great."

Her friend eyed Marcela curiously before answering. "Nothing yet. I've got some ground chuck out thawing." Sandy turned toward her opened door and sniffed. "I can't smell anything." She turned back to her friend. "You sure you smell something from my apartment?"

Marcela nodded. Shrugged.

"Thought you didn't care for meat?"

"I don't," Marcela replied, feeling slightly confused, because something did indeed smell very good, even activating her salivary glands.

They chatted a few more minutes, Marcela not mentioning anything about her trip or the peculiar body changes, instead convincing her neighbor that she was fine except for a little PMS. They agreed to a movie early in the coming week. Then they hugged goodbye, Marcela finding the actual physical contact unsettling.

She closed the door to Sandy, puzzled by her reaction to physical contact. She'd always enjoyed hugging and being hugged.

***

Running...

Running...looking for something that's close but stays just out of reach.

The slick, muddy paths of the rainforest replaced by sidewalks of asphalt and stone, her hunt taking her into the concrete jungle now, but her quest unchanged.

Searching...

Always searching...

***

Marcela woke up just as it was getting dark, the night sounds of the city coming through her window, which she'd left open for some air. But she found it stifling in her apartment tonight. She got up and stretched, not bothering to dress, feeling unusually restless, but intrigued by the mystery of the dream. Running through the city instead of the forest had put an interesting new twist on things, but it didn't answer any of her questions. What was she searching for? No matter how hard she thought about it, she had no clue.

Still naked, she again examined herself in the mirror. The skin mottling seemed much more pronounced; and there was no doubt now that her breasts and hip curves were disappearing. Marcela knew she should feel much more alarmed, should consider calling her doctor-- perhaps the body changes related to some kind of undetected damage from the park attack. But she didn't really believe that at all. No. For some intuitive reason, she felt no real deep anxiety about the changes, only a little curiosity. They felt right. She thought again about Mambo Ranice, and felt that somehow the mystery of the dreams were directly related to her body transformation.

What was she searching for in the city?

Later, on a whim, Marcela clicked on the TV, hoping to hear on the news that the heat wave was going to break soon. As the picture appeared, she realized she hadn't had the TV on since coming home from the hospital. And the rape, over two weeks ago now. My God, it seemed much longer. Already the details of that night were growing fuzzy in her memory. In fact, unlike her old self, she was spending less and less time in the past, more concerned with the here and now. Everything present tense.

The anchorwoman had been interviewing a police department lieutenant. The detective was talking about specific episodes of violence within the general city chaos--gang behavior.

Marcela turned up the sound.

"...That's right, Cheryl," the policeman was nodding. "It has escalated, proliferating from the North Central projects. Laughing Death, the apparent dominant gang now apparently with hundreds of members, has spread out, muggings on the Muni, robberies in convenience stores in the northern suburbs, some members even moving down into the park. Several reported robberies and rapes."

The anchorwoman used the police department

spokesman as a lead-in to a reporter at St. Mary's Hospital. He was interviewing an apparent gang victim. The young man, a cyclist, was lying with a leg in traction, his face bruised and swollen. He'd been attacked along the Westside biking trail, not far from the site of Marcela's attack. The reporter held out the mic as the victim painfully described the experience--they'd stolen his wallet, bike, and beaten him badly.

Then back to the anchorwoman, Cheryl, who summarized the new wave of terror by the Laughing Death Gang, showing a still shot of a gang member in colors. The boy was wearing a black bandanna on his head and a black windbreaker with a white caricature of a grinning skull over the right breast.

"They don't care if their colors identify them," Cheryl concluded. "They seem to want the notoriety."

As Marcela watched the broadcast, she probably should have felt some anxiety after realizing who her attackers had been and the hazard they still presented in the park. But she experienced no fear, only a growing restlessness, an inability to concentrate on anything pertaining to the past. At the end of the newscast she switched off the TV, and despite the muggy temperature and obvious danger, she went out. But other than wandering about aimlessly in the steamy night, she saw nothing, encountered no one, returning home a little before daybreak, dropping down her bed and drifting off into an exhausted sleep, clutching her cool silver pendant for comfort. Her tired mind barely registered that the once smooth sphere had grown four tiny legs and the beginnings of a head and tail...

***

In the crotch of the tree she stretches for a moment or two, glancing about into the dark humid night, listening carefully and sniffing in all directions--deciding everything is normal before dropping to the ground eight feet below, landing lightly on all four paws. She begins to move quickly through the heavy undergrowth, slipping past large leaves extending out into her path, pausing every now and then to sample a specific, strengthening scent, before hurrying along quickly...searching, searching.

She follows the path to where it crosses a concrete path, a bike path, and she realizes she's back in the concrete jungle--a park.

Then, she stops abruptly, sniffing the muggy, scented air and inadvertently her mouth waters with the recognition: prey.

Her lithe body seems to shrink as she hunkers down and begins to stalk seriously, sampling the air as she moves, but actively searching now with her amber colored eyes.

There, ahead on the bike path--three figures, all dressed in black.

Effortlessly she leaps up out of sight, up into a nearby tree, coming to rest above the prey, her tail twitching out of control as she waits for them to walk below, unable to suppress the joy of the hunt from rumbling up from deep in her chest, making the distinctive hoarse coughing sound of her kind.

The three figures are grouped closely in place, searching for the source of the odd sound, their fear smell thick in the moist air.

Still she hesitates for another moment, peering down through the leaves, making another coughing-growl as she tenses for her attack...

***

The evening news was full of the ferocious vigilante attack on the Laughing Death Gang members in the park--the three boys almost torn apart by their attackers--the authorities estimating at least half a dozen suspects armed with some kind of sharp knives.

Marcela, lying on the couch, watched, but was only marginally interested in the gruesome details of the apparent ambush of the three teenaged boys.

The phone interrupted the program.

It was Peter.

"I've been thinking, Babe," the unfaithful bastard said, using the hated nickname. "Maybe we were too hasty. I've had second thoughts about our separation."

Separation--a temporary state?

"Maybe we should talk," he continued.

Marcela paused a moment before shrugging to herself. "Okay," she agreed in a hoarse voice.

"Are you running tonight?"

"Yes, in a few minutes."

"Good," he said, his voice rising slightly in pitch. "I'll meet you in the park. We can jog together and talk. You'd like that, right, Babe?"

Oh, she'd like that, yes, indeed. Marcela coughed, then whispered, "That will be fine, Peter. Can hardly wait."

She looked down, feeling the vibration, an almost purring sensation against her chest where the silver jaguar pendant rested.

STORY NOTES

Time can heal all pain. Well, that's how the saying goes, anyway. It's a nice, happy little expression but not exactly true. Sure, physical pain will fade as the days, weeks, months, and years go by, but psychological pain usually doesn't go away quite as easily and time really doesn't have much to do with it. It's people who heal themselves, I think. Humans are extremely adaptable and no matter what a man or woman goes through, their minds have wonderful survival mechanism that allows them to deal with the pain, anger, and grief and move on with life. We never forget though.

Never.

Marcella Transmuting is a story that I co-wrote with my friend and sidekick, Gene O'Neill and at its heart it's a story about change. And revenge, I suppose. Bad things happen to people all the time and it inevitably changes them for the better or worse. Some can rise above the anger and turn the other cheek, while others can't. Either way, they change and become different people from whoever they thought they were before.

When you talk about someone changing in a horror

story, most readers and writers automatically think werewolves and full moons but Gene and I wanted to come up with something different. Gene doesn't like to follow the rule or the familiar tropes of the genre so we settled on using Voodoo as our catalyst of change, thinking that was something strange enough for us to work with. After all, Gene and I are a little strange ourselves. They don't call us the Butch and Sundance of Horror for nothing you know; but that's another story for another day…

ALL THAT GLITTERS...

"Mr. Carson... my associate and I have a problem."

Brad Carson, killer for hire for the Chicago Mafia, was five feet eleven inches tall, and two hundred and ten pounds of solid muscle. He had dark black hair cropped short on top, but grown long and tied up in a ponytail at the back. Dressed in a pullover gray sweater, black jeans and a brand new pair of high-top Doc Martins, he looked casual but undeniably tough. Carson had a real bad feeling about this meeting, and was in no mood to screw around.

"Hey, don't we all," he sarcastically replied. "Get on with it fella. I haven't got all night."

The man who'd spoken was in his late fifties, fat, balding, and had a flat face and a block-shaped head. He spoke with a slight German accent. The other man in the room was around forty, trim, had shoulder length sandy-brown hair and nervous shifty eyes that constantly roamed the room.

Without warning, the thin man suddenly bolted up and nervously blurted, "You won't believe it, man... This'll blow your mind. We found a gold mine, you see, but now everything's all fucked up. Everything!"

"You found a *what?*" Carson asked.

"A gold mine, man. An honest to freakin' God, gold mine. It's worth a fortune. Millions, man... maybe *billions*."

Carson asked the most obvious question that popped into his mind. "And this... is a problem?"

"No, that's not the problem, man. I told you already. Everything's all fucked up... Aren't you *listening*? We go and find a lake of gold and can't get at it. That's the *freakin'* problem."

"A lake of Gold?" Carson turned toward the fat man still sitting stoically on his left. "What's he babbling about?"

The fat man ran his pudgy fingers through his thinning hair, then held up his hands as in mock surrender. He was clearly frustrated but trying to stay calm.

"Let's slow down a minute. We should introduce ourselves. My name is Karl Stein and my rather excitable colleague here is Roger Bishop. Incredible as it may sound, Mr. Bishop and I have indeed found, for a lack of a better term, a deposit of liquid gold. Bear with me for a moment and I'll get to all that. There are a few things you need to understand first. Okay?"

This time Carson was too stunned to respond. *Liquid gold? Were these guys fucking with him? Did such a thing even exist?* Mr. Stein took his silence as a sign of compliance and carried on.

"This began about seventeen months ago, last May the tenth to be exact. Mr. Bishop and I are both geologists who were employed by the State of Illinois to do some research in an area known as the Lincoln Hills

Karst. Karst is simply a Yugoslavian term describing an area with natural Limestone bedrock. These areas all have similar characteristics, such as sinkholes, underground caverns..."

"Tell him about the monster," Bishop interrupted. "No, better yet, show him the pictures, man. That no good dirty rotten son of a *freakin'*..."

"Easy, Roger," Stein silenced him. "Let me tell this, okay?"

"Whatever, man... whatever." The thin man shrugged his shoulders and sulked back into his chair.

What was Carson supposed to make of that? Had Bishop really said... *monster?* And they had *pictures?* This meeting was getting weirder by the second. Carson wasn't sure he wanted to hear the rest, but decided to stick it out a few more minutes. Stein carried on with his story, barely missing a beat.

"So we were working in the Lincoln Hills region, mapping some of the caves in the area, when suddenly we stumbled into every treasure hunter's dream come true. There was gold everywhere we looked.

"Not gold nuggets, but something that nearly defies description. *Liquid Gold!* We believe a super-heated geothermal pocket lies directly beneath the cave floor. Maybe it's something volcanic? Regardless... *something* in the immediate area is hot enough to have liquefied a rather substantial deposit of gold. We tested a small sample, and it's not pure gold... there are a lot of other compounds mixed with it, but Roger was correct when he appraised its value earlier. It's worth millions. If, that is, we can ever get our hands on it."

"I take it this is where your problem comes into the picture?" correctly guessed Carson.

"Exactly. Since our discovery, we legally purchased the farmland and wooded area surrounding our particular cave, and we also received a mining permit from the State. We should be on easy street by now... but obviously we're not. Someone is hiding in our woods, guarding the entrance to the cave, and sabotaging us. They've already murdered seven men we hired to help us start reclaiming the gold."

"Why don't you call the police?" Carson asked.

"No way! We can't go to the cops, man." Bishop nervously shook his head, waiting until Stein gave him the okay, before explaining their dilemma. "The land is legit, sure, but the money we used to buy it wasn't. It costs a whole whack of cash to front an operation like this, man. We didn't have squat, so we talked your mob friends into helping us.

"They fronted the money to buy the land, greased a few government palms to get our mining permit, and bought all the necessary tools, supplies, and whatever else we needed. Now we mine the gold, then sell it to them for less than half market price. They get filthy rich reselling it on the black market, but Karl and I still get our millions without any of the hassles. It was a cut and dried deal, man. *Cut and freakin' dried*... until that psycho monster showed up."

"So you can understand why we can't run to the police," Stein interjected. "Like I said, my associate and I have a problem... so we've come to you for a solution. We'll give you fifteen thousand dollars. Cash, of course. Half now... half later. Can you help us?"

It wasn't an easy question and Carson certainly wasn't going to rush into making a stupid decision. Something about all this was wrong — something he just couldn't place. He needed the cash, but all the money in the world wouldn't do him any good if he got himself killed. Whoever was killing the mineworkers obviously was good at what he did, so killing him wouldn't be easy. And he would certainly be on guard, and more than ready to defend himself. No, this sounded a little too crazy. Carson didn't want anything to do with it.

"Sorry guys... It's too damn risky."

His decision made, he stood up to leave. He noticed the look of spreading panic on Stein and Bishop's faces and said, "Don't worry... I'm not the only game in town. Call your contact man. He'll probably set you up with either Charlie Barnes or Jack Clinton. They're both good."

The best action always seemed to get split between him and these two rivals - Barnes and Clinton. Carson considered them both closet psycho's, but even he had to grudgingly admit that they were damn good at their jobs.

He turned on his heels and began to walk out of the room. From behind him, Stein stopped him cold by saying, "We already have, Mr. Carson."

"What?" he asked, spinning back around. "Which one?"

"Both, actually."

"Well, hell... that settles it. If you think I'm gonna go get my ass shot off just because the first two people you wanted turned you down, you're..."

"They didn't turn us down" Stein interrupted. "They both accepted. Rather eagerly, if I remember right."

Yeah, they would, Carson thought. This kind of thing was right up those two lunatics alley. He had to ask.

"What happened?"

Mr. Bishop pulled a brown envelope out of his

briefcase and flicked it into Carson's hands. Before he even opened it, Carson knew what he was going to find inside. Photographs.

Carson removed the stack of color prints and immediately wished he hadn't. The damage inflicted to the bodies in the photos was so incredible he could hardly believe his eyes. Carson had been in the killing business for a long time and to him violence was an everyday companion. He'd thought he'd seen everything — until now. Who the hell were they dealing with here?

"Are you trying to tell me that these... these lumps of hamburger, are Barnes and Clinton?" he asked in shock.

"Only Barnes," Bishop replied. "Some of the other men we sent into the mine, too. What's left of them, anyway. We don't know what happened to Clinton. He went into that freakin' cave, but he never came back out."

"These men weren't killed... They've been *mutilated*. Have you considered the possibility it might be an animal that attacked them? Maybe wild dogs are living in the cave? Maybe it's a bear?"

Bishop was quick to respond. "I told you earlier, man... It's a monster. It's some kind of kick ass, mother *freakin'* monster!"

"Oh shut up Roger... please," Stein begged. "Don't make this any more complicated than it already is. As for your animal theory Mr. Carson, we initially thought the same thing, but there are no animal tracks anywhere. With each murder, we find a set of human footprints walking away from the carnage. They disappear at the entrance of the cave. No, it's a man all right. A maniac for sure, as those pictures can attest, but a man nonetheless. What if we offer twenty-thousand?"

"I'm still not interested. Goodbye."

"I'm sorry to hear that... but not as sorry as Mr. Scarpelli will be. He said to say this was a personal favor you'd be doing for him. Of course, if you're too busy, I can…"

"Shut the fuck up!" Carson exploded, having heard more than enough. "Don't try playing the heavy with me, fat boy. You ain't got what it takes."

Arlo Scarpelli was the head of the Mafia family in Chicago. When Scarpelli asked for a personal favor, there weren't many people stupid enough to turn him down. If what Stein was saying was true, Carson might be about to make the biggest mistake of his life. He went with his gut feeling anyway.

"You're full of shit, Stein. You and your little sidekick here don't have nothing to do with Scarpelli. Right from the start something didn't feel right about this meeting and now I think I've finally got it. You're on your own... aren't you? Scarpelli would never let a couple of schmucks like you handle such an important hit. Oh sure, you might have greased somebody in the family to get them to contact me, and maybe they're even kicking in some money, but that's as far as it goes. Scarpelli doesn't know what you're up to. If he did, he'd whack both you clowns and take all the gold for himself. See you later guys, I'm out of here. Good luck on the monster hunt."

Before Carson had taken three steps toward the door, Stein was shouting in panic, "Okay... you win. We are on our own, but don't leave. Just hear me out... okay? Everything else we've said is true. The gold is there. I *swear* it is! I apologize for the charade, but we needed your help. We're desperate, Mr. Carson. Name your price... Okay? Just please don't leave."

This was more like it. Carson still didn't like the hit, but he was far too greedy to pass up a chance like this.

"All right Stein... you got yourself a killer, but I want more than twenty grand. I want a hundred, and not a god-damned nickel less, you hear me?"

"Done" Stein said without hesitation, an obvious look of relief on his face. "Same terms. You get fifty-thousand now... fifty later." He quickly counted out five thick stacks of cash and placed the money into Carson's hands before he changed his mind. "Any questions?"

"Yeah, when do you want this done?"

Stein and Bishop huddled together for a moment, then Bishop asked, "What are your plans for tomorrow, man?"

***

Carson was walking three paces behind Stein and Bishop on the narrow wooded trail, when they came to a sudden stop. The trail ahead continued on, and as far as Carson could tell, nothing was impeding their way.

"What's the problem?" he asked.

"This is as far as we go, man," Bishop whispered, the tension and nervousness in his voice almost palatable. "For some reason, the son of a bitch draws the line right here. We can party all day here where we're standing, but step past that big boulder ahead there... You're freakin' monster meat."

"Would you stop that?" Stein glared at his partner. "You know perfectly well it's a man we're dealing with here."

Carson wished they would both shut up. They weren't

exactly building his confidence with all their crazy talk. How had he managed to get himself into this mess, anyway? More importantly, how was he going to get himself out?

A full week had passed since their meeting. Stein and Bishop had been all gung-ho to race down here the very next day but Carson had balked. It was his ass on the line, and he wasn't going anywhere until he was good and ready. In this case, ready meant getting his hands on some very serious firepower. He'd be damned if he were going to play one on one with some backwoods maniac without being prepared. It had been difficult getting his hands on an untraceable Magnum 44 handgun and a Heckler and Koch HK-51 machine gun on such short notice, difficult but not impossible. When Carson had said he wanted serious firepower, he'd meant it.

Stein and Bishop had picked him up in a nondescript Plymouth Voyager mini-van. They had taken the Eisenhower Expressway out of the city, then caught the I-55 southwest towards the state line. They had travelled some two hundred and sixty miles in four hours, before pulling to a stop at a dilapidated farmhouse on the outskirts of the town of Alton, Illinois. Carson's had felt quite good on the drive down, but now that it was time to earn his money, his confidence was wilting rapidly as the sun slowly began to set.

"I've got more guns back in the van," Carson stalled. "Why don't you both come with me? The three of us stand a better chance of taking this guy out, than me on my own."

"I don't think so, Mr. Carson," Stein answered, rapidly shaking his head. "This is your line of expertise... not ours. We're going to stay right here."

Bishop, turning white as a ghost at the mere mention of going into the cave, for once never even responded. Like it or not, Carson was on his own.

"Tell me again what happened to Jack Clinton?" he asked Stein, while rechecking his machine gun and ammunition clips.

"We're not really sure. All the other men who went in, we found deposited right back here. This is the spot where we took all of those ghastly pictures. Mr. Clinton entered the cave two weeks ago and there's been no sign of him since. There's a chance he's still alive, but it's not very likely."

"What does this guy want, anyway? Have you been in contact with him at all?"

"No, not a word. He's carved obscene pictures into a few of the victim's bellies, but there's no apparent method to his madness. We don't know why he's doing this? Maybe you can ask him... before you kill the bastard. Pump a bullet through his twisted brain for us, okay?"

Carson nodded and took a couple of tentative steps along the trail. He was as ready as he was ever going to be.

"Good luck, man," Bishop said from behind him. Then in a barely audible whisper, said, "You can bet your freakin' ass... You're gonna *need* it."

***

Stein had instructed Carson to follow the trail to a shallow stream. Just across the stream, he'd find a path sloping up and away to his right. The entrance to the cave was at the top of the slope, where the ground leveled off.

It might have been his imagination, but Carson was sure the forest had become quieter. As if every plant and animal in the area were collectively holding their breath, awaiting the outcome of the battle ahead. He took a deep breath to calm his nerves, and started moving forward again.

It wasn't long until he spotted the stream about one hundred paces away. He could just barely make out the noise of its water gently gurgling downstream. It would normally be a calming sound, peaceful, but tonight it filled him with dread. Soft as it was, the flowing water would still easily cover any telltale noises of someone trying to sneak up on him.

With every step closer to the stream, the noise, as well as his anxiety, steadily increased. Carson's heart was pounding so hard, that by the time he made it successfully to the edge of the shallow stream, it felt like a sledgehammer banging inside his chest. The journey had taken two minutes, but had felt more like two hours. Although extremely nerve racking; so far, things had been relatively uneventful. Things wouldn't stay that way, though. Carson could feel the approaching danger like an icy January wind. Something bad was about to happen and he knew it was going to happen soon.

Carson had no idea how accurate his prediction would be. He had only waded a few feet into the knee-deep dark water, when his feet were suddenly swept out from underneath him. He barely had time to draw a deep breath and register the presence of a massive man rising above him, before landing on his back, submerging beneath the froth.

In his panic, Carson sprayed off a few rounds from

the rapid-firing Heckler and Koch, but the shots were wild, more of a reflex action then any real attempt at defending himself. He quickly tried to get his head above water and regain his feet, but a large hand crashed into his chest, pinning him to the rocky bottom. Carson tried to pry the assailant's hand away and roll loose, but whoever it was, they were as strong as a bull.

Carson's lungs were already screaming for oxygen. If he couldn't fight his way to the surface soon, there would be no fight left in him. He didn't want to die like this. The water was cold, dark, and so murky that Carson couldn't see the hand on his chest, much less the face of the man who was killing him. The machine gun was of no good for this kind of in close fighting. His only option was the Magnum 44. The Magnum was one of the most powerful handguns around and would make a mess of this madman from this range.

Carson somehow managed to wiggle the handgun out from under his belt. He was forced to use his left hand to fire the weapon but from an arm's length away, it was virtually impossible to miss. He had a horrific vision flash through his oxygen-starved brain, of pulling the trigger over and over, but the gun being too waterlogged to fire. Fortunately, the Magnum performed flawlessly, the first bullet exploding out of the chamber toward where Carson believed his assailant's chest to be.

The hand pinning Carson lifted away, as the deafening blast must have scored a bull's eye, tossing the large man backward. Carson had barely broken the surface and gulped a few mouthfuls of air; hadn't even had time to wipe the water out of his stinging eyes, when amazingly, the attacker was back on top of him pushing him beneath the water again. What kind of a man could take a .44 caliber slug point blank to the chest, then get back up to continue fighting? He should have been dead instantly, floating downstream with a six-inch hole shredding his back. Unlikely as it seemed, maybe the shot had missed.

Before Carson could fire again, the man drove a fist into Carson's face. The powerful blow stunned him enough that he fumbled and lost his grip on the gun. He was making a feeble attempt at recovering it when the next blow landed solidly on the left side of his jaw. The world exploded in a star burst behind Carson's eyes, and then everything went black. For the next minute, he faded in and out of consciousness, wondering how he seemed able to breathe underwater all of a sudden. He was too dazed to realize he'd been lifted from the shallow stream and was now being dragged by his heels up the sloping path toward the entrance to the cave.

Through unfocused eyes, Carson managed to finally catch a glimpse of his adversary, and realized how this psycho might possibly have been able to stand up after the direct hit from the Magnum. For some unfathomable reason, the huge man dragging Carson into the darkness of the cave was wearing what appeared to be a suit of polished golden armor. Carson tried to make some sense of what he'd seen, but his eyes rolled up into their sockets and his mind drifted into the blissful arms of darkness.

***

Carson awakened drenched in sweat, in the grip of the worst headache of his life. His jaw also hurt like hell. The rest of him felt relatively okay, with nothing more serious than a few cuts and bruises. Carson had no way of knowing how long he'd been unconscious, or what had become of the man in the golden armor.

He was lying on his back inside of a crudely constructed steel cage. Through the bars, he could see the rough limestone walls and ceiling, and realized he was inside of the cavern. He felt a blistering heat beneath his back and when he rolled over to check out the source, he was shocked.

The cage he was in was suspended fifteen feet in the air by a steel cable that disappeared into the shadow shrouded ceiling. Below Carson, and obviously the source of all the light and heat in the cavern, was the lake of liquid gold.

With the exception of one small area near a bolted wooden door, the entire cavern appeared to be submerged in this decadent sea of unimaginable wealth. The gold glowed with a bright, ominous aura that could only be described as heavenly. Great geysers of the precious metal rolled on the surface, then shot into the air on currents of super-heated steam and venting gases. It was a breathtaking sight, and Carson had never witnessed anything like it.

With a loud thump, the only door into the chamber was thrown wide open and in walked the man Carson had fought with. When he came into full view, and Carson finally had a chance to really take a good look, he let out a scream of horror and amazement. This man, if that was in fact what Carson was looking at, wasn't wearing a suit of armor after all — in fact, he wasn't wearing anything whatsoever. He was completely sealed in a cocoon of gold. No, that wasn't right either, because there were no breathing holes or cut out apertures to see from. Carson couldn't believe his eyes. This wasn't simply a man covered in gold, but a living statue of a man, made entirely *of* gold.

He was nearly as impressive of a sight as the lake he guarded over, his sculpted image shining with the same inner brilliance. He turned and looked up at his captive, smiling a large toothy grin, which Carson would have thought impossible. How could a creature made of solid gold, have the ability to perform a flexible maneuver such as smiling?

"You have many questions, I'm sure," the golden man said in a gravely, yet perfectly decipherable voice.

Carson was too stunned to speak. Was this really happening? Maybe he was still unconscious and simply dreaming this craziness. Finally he built up his courage and asked, "Who are you? I mean... what are you?"

"I am exactly what you see, a fully functioning man, who's all that you are... and more. I've simply evolved differently than you. Obviously, what with our similar features, we must have paddled around together in the same primordial soup back when the world was young. But from there we chose our own paths."

"But that's..." Carson was about to say impossible, but the last thing he wanted to do was piss this creature off by ridiculously denying its obvious existence.

"Enough of this pointless talk, it's time for you to die," the golden man said, walking over to the wall on his left where he casually began turning a rusty handle. To Carson's horror, the cage he sat within, slowly began lowering toward the molten metal below.

"No! *Wait*. I'll make you a deal," Carson pleaded. "Let me go and I'll make sure no one ever bothers you again. I'll kill Stein and Bishop myself if you want. They're only interested in the gold and all the--"

"Gold? What gold is that?"

Carson thought he was kidding. "The lake, of course."

"This... lake, as you call it, isn't made of gold," he said incredulously. "It has similar properties, but believe me, it's not gold."

"What is it, then?"

"Actually, it's my people... my family, if you will."

"Your *what!*" Carson asked, shocked to the core.

"It's hard to explain. Why don't I show you?"

The golden man raised his hands to his mouth and blew a short high note, which echoed within the confined room. Almost immediately, a head popped out of the molten liquid, quickly followed by dozens of others. Soon people were walking out of the lake to stand near their leader. With every new body, the level of the lake dropped a few more inches. With mounting amazement, Carson realized that these people weren't coming out from being in the golden liquid — they *were* the liquid. It took ten minutes, but eventually every ounce was used up, and the cavern was filled to capacity with gleaming people.

"Now do you understand?" their leader asked. "We live as one entity within the lake, but can separate and solidify at will. We've lived countless millennia within this planet's molten core. It wasn't until a massive underground tremor caused a shifting in the tectonic plates that a gateway opened between our subterranean world and yours. Even after we learned of your existence, we still only sought to be left alone, to live in peace, but things seem destined to change for us.

"Unfortunately, violence is the only thing you humans understand, so we thought if we killed a few of the men who trespassed in our cave, we'd be left alone. Those two idiots who sent you just won't go away though."

"Release me and I'll kill them right now. They'll never bother you again."

"Easy, friend. I don't want them killed. If I did, I'd have killed them myself long ago. We have a *new* plan."

He paused to make that high-pitched echoing sound again. The multitude of golden people began to melt back down to join with one another again. Soon, the original golden man stood alone again beside the molten lake. He slowly started turning the rusty handle again; continuing Carson's decent. He ignored Carson's screams, revealing their master plan as he cranked.

"We need those idiots to keep bringing us more people. How else can we build our army? You see... We've decided to expand our horizons and take over your surface world. We've learned that your race is powerless to defend against us. You can't shoot us… the bullet passes through us as it would through water. Bend, break, or explode us apart... we flow back together whole again. We are *indestructible*.

"Imagine for a moment, the awesome sight of our golden army flowing through the city streets, assimilating the human population into our ranks as we go. As soon as we have enough men, we'll launch an offensive. Don't worry... we can use a man with skills like yours. When I said I was going to kill you... I didn't mean *permanently*. You're one of the lucky ones. You have been chosen to join us. In fact, you came highly recommended."

"Recommended? By *who?*"

He clapped his hands together and one head popped out from the surface of the bubbling lake.

"Hey, buddy... long time no see," the new arrival spoke, swimming up and grabbing onto the bottom edge of Carson's cage as it slowly descended to within a few inches of this strange unknown species of molten people. Even in his semi-liquid form, Carson immediately recognized who it was. It was Jack Clinton, the other Mafia hit man who'd been missing for over two weeks.

"We're one big happy family down here, Carson old buddy," shouted the entity who had once been Jack Clinton. "One big happy family... join us."

"*NOOOOO...*" Carson screamed, as the first pain-filled wave of the fiery golden liquid touched his skin.

As the cage continued to descend, the molten liquid washed over Carson's feet, his ankles, and then his legs — melting his flesh inch by agonizing inch. Soon, the flesh and blood that had been Brad Carson was no more, but that didn't mean he was gone. Changed, certainly, but gone, no. He had joined with another race of beings and was already helping them with their battle plans. Carson may have lost his humanity, but in doing so he'd gained a whole new perspective on life — a *golden* perspective.

Story Notes

I've always been a fan of Jules Verne and his fantastical tales of inner space interested me just as much as all the outer space fiction I was reading. There was a time back in my high school days that I was determined to write an adventure novel that took place within the earth's core. I wasn't shooting for a *Journey To The Center Of The Earth*, like Mr. Verne had envisioned, complete with tropical plants and giant prehistoric dinosaurs running around, but I did want to write something scary set in a deep cave system that a group of adventurers were going to explore miles beneath the surface. I never did write that book; never even started it really, because I could never figure out what was waiting for my spelunkers down at the bottom of the cave. The best idea I remember coming up with was having them being attacked by a group of humanoid looking cannibals who were blind from never seeing the light of the sun. It might have been decent, or it might have been trash, but I'll never know now.

The point is I still love adventure and horror stories set beneath the earth's surface and although *All That*

Glitters... is one of my early stories, it's one that I'm still quite fond of. Not only did I make an attempt to write my cave story, but I also was trying to stretch my imagination a little and not stick to the horror genre. This is a horror story, sure, but it has a lot of fantasy and science fiction swimming around down in the deep end of the Lake of Gold too. I had hardly written a word of science fiction and it felt good to toss my hat into the ring, even if it was just a little.

UNNATURAL SELECTION

...It is like confessing a murder.

Those words still chill me to the bone, every time I think of them. They were the words uttered by my famous ancestor Charles Darwin, when he revealed to the world what he knew to be true about evolution, accurately predicting the uproar and ramifications of his theories would surely incite. Even before the first copy of his masterpiece, On the Origin of Species by Means of Natural Selection rolled off the press in 1859, a storm of controversy was brewing over his perceived audacity at challenging contemporary beliefs about the creation of life here on earth.

My name is Dr. Ian Darwin and although I'm honored to meet you, I wish it were under different, more pleasant circumstances. I'm a 68 year-old professor with doctorates in both Biology and Anthropology. Retired professor, I should say, for three years now, my thirty-six year tenure dropped like the proverbial hot stone to make way for "a new breed of teacher," as it was rudely stated to me. A new breed — rather fitting, in light of what we've come here to discuss, wouldn't you say? Enough of me though, let's get back on track. Let's talk about Charles.

Just to set the record straight, my great-great-grandfather never said that human beings evolved from apes or monkeys. It was the multitude of people reading and interpreting his words for themselves that said such a thing. Believe it or not, from everything I've read in his private notes — those musty smelling leather bound journals handed down to me from my father - Charles seemed more inclined to consider us descended from headless hermaphroditic squids. I kid you not!

Regardless what creature spawned us, whether we were swinging through treetops or submerged beneath the primordial swamps, somehow we arrived, evolved according to our environment to become what you see reflected in the mirror today.

Homo Sapiens.

We are, for the time being at least, perched upon the top rung of the food chain, the unchallenged master here on this planet. A creature of supreme intelligence and cunning, capable of astounding mental and physical acts duplicated by no other species past or present, but let's not get too high on ourselves.

It would be intrinsically wrong, dangerously audacious even, to assume our species will always remain as the "top dog" on this ever-changing overcrowded kennel we share with so many progressively — some might argue, aggressively — evolving breeds. We're not as different as you might think from our less egotistical neighbors. One way or another, we all eat, sleep, and breathe. We live, we die, all sharing the same urge to procreate, to continue on our kind long after we are gone. We feel warmth, pain, confusion, and perhaps the most common emotion of all — fear. Ah yes... *FEAR*. The tie that binds!

Now we're getting somewhere.

My great-great-grandfather knew fear. He knew it well, my friend, and if you can keep a secret I've a strange story to tell, a story that never has — and never will — be included in any of the history books. Interested?

It's been well documented how Charles' voyage aboard the HMS Beagle directly lead him to formulate his theories concerning natural selection, but almost no one has heard the real story of what happened on the Galapagos Islands in the fall of 1835. It's true that it was here he began to form a coherent view of what ultimately would become his legacy, but it was also here that something triggered the horrible nightmares Charles would be plagued with throughout the rest of his days. Dreams and visions so terrible, so consuming, he hid them away from the prying eyes of the world in case someone discovered the source of his fear and disregarded his life's work as the ravings of a madman.

To understand Charles' fear, his hidden obsession, you must first understand the man himself. Charles was a twenty-two-year-old young man freshly graduated from Cambridge University, deeply religious and heading for a life in the clergy before accepting the unpaid post of naturalist aboard the Beagle. He did not in the least doubt the literal truth of every word in the Bible. In fact, he saw his job as a grand opportunity to substantiate the Bible, hoping to find evidence of the Flood, and the first appearance of all created things, exactly as they were set out in the book of Genesis. He was young and impetuous, looking at the grueling ocean voyage through rose-colored glasses, fantasizing some sort of heroic adventure. Reality would soon set him straight. Day after day, year after year living in cramped quarters on the high seas has a way of testing even the most ardent of a man's beliefs. Charles' beliefs would be more than simply tested, but rather, shaken to their very foundation.

Let's step back in time, shall we, step aboard the sturdy mahogany planks of the HMS Beagle, a relatively small ninety feet in length, ten gun brig under the competent leadership of Captain Robert FitzRoy, and join Charles nearly four years into his five year voyage of discovery. The Galapagos Islands: just another port of call in this long journey. For Charles though, it was a magical place, a naturalist's paradise — a place of rugged beauty and hidden secrets that would simultaneously ignite a fire of passion within his brilliant mind, and construct an icy prison of fear to permanently cage his troubled soul...

***

It happened on October 15, 1835. The Beagle was moored near a black-lava shoal just off the western tip of Tower Island - one of the smaller, outer-islands in the Galapagos chain. The midday equatorial sun beat directly down upon the small landing party that consisted of Charles, Captain FitzRoy, and four crewmen currently in good favor, as they prepared to go ashore for a friendly afternoon excursion. They'd been scouring these volcanically formed islands for a month already, having arrived September 15 from Patagonia and the West Coast of South America. They planned a rare social call, to visit an American whaling vessel whose crew had been kind enough to provide them with three casks of fresh water, which they'd needed badly, and a large bucket of onions. FitzRoy felt a visit to thank the ship's captain personally, was in order.

Tower Island, or Isla Genovesa as it was known, was a mirror image of most of the other Galapagos Islands - black lava outcroppings, skeletal thin brushwood that clung to the rocky terrain, and sparse green flora that poked up through black sand so hot it burned their feet even through thick boots.

Charles immediately sensed that something wasn't quite right there, something was different from on the other islands. It only took him a few minutes to figure out what was so strange. It was the animals — or lack of them — that captured his attention. Everywhere else on the chain of islands, the wildlife was abundant, literally teeming with a multitude of unique species. The word Galapagos is Spanish for giant tortoises, and the 400 lb. massive creatures were virtually everywhere, slowly making their way to and from the inland watering holes. There were also iguanas of all colors and sizes constantly scurrying underfoot, birds too diverse and numerous to mention, and all manner of other life, big and small, crawling, slithering, and flying. But, for some reason, none of them were present there on Tower Island. There, everything was quiet, seemingly vacant.

Charles was the only person to notice the anomaly, the other members of the landing party in too jovial a mood thinking about the food and ale that awaited them at the whaler's camp to be concerned about the absence of a few turtles and finches. They'd spotted several large tortoise shells along their route, but no one save for Charles was perplexed as to why the shells were cracked and broken, the carcasses of the noble animals nowhere to be found.

It wasn't until they'd walked half the small island, with a steep climb over a large, black volcanic ridge still separating them from the bay where the American ship waited at anchor, that Captain Fitzroy brought their happy march to a halt. He finally felt the same disturbance, the same unspoken uneasiness that had been making Charles' hair bristle on the back of his neck since he'd left the relative safety of the Beagle nearly an hour earlier. FitzRoy warned them to keep their eyes open, that something wasn't right ... perhaps feeling with a sixth sense the electric buzz of imminent danger, but not aware what the problem was, or what to do about it.

Charles was the first to reach the top of the ridge. What he saw below him in the American's makeshift camp, was an assault on his very sanity — a scene so far removed from his Christian sensibilities that he'd been positive it was a nightmare, an exhaustion-fueled postcard glimpse into his conscience's interpretation of Dante's Inferno. Never had Charles seen such carnage, such bloodshed, in one place before. It was as if they had peered in the front door of the Devil's Butcher Shop, a ghastly human abattoir ludicrously misplaced in that beautiful tropical setting. There were bodies everywhere he looked, or parts of bodies, to be more accurate. A severed arm was half-buried in a drift of black sand. A torn and twisted leg propped against a wooden stool still wearing a crimson-streaked brown leather boot. A disembodied head stared forever out to sea with gray jelly-like brains still oozing from the ragged hole where its nose should have been. Those atrocities and a great many more waited on the beach for Charles and his companions as they stumbled down the far side of the ridge in muted shock.

The ocean-cooled air seemed thicker somehow, the sickening heavy tang of salty-copper making every breath a chore to swallow. What had happened here? Inspecting the chaos, FitzRoy was convinced that a war had been fought or a savage mutiny committed, the rebellious crew slaughtering the whaling ship's officers as well as most of their mates. Neither explanation had made much sense to Charles. Surely they'd have heard the thundering noise of a fierce battle being fought, and the large whaling vessel was still in the bay; lifeless now, a ghost ship with no would-be mutineers left to ever hoist its rusty anchor or lay claim to its cargo of slowly rotting blubber.

Gathering his courage, Charles inspected the mutilated bodies closer, with a scientist's eye, not as a clergyman. He quickly discovered the horrifying truth. These men hadn't died by musket balls, or swords. Their bodies weren't blown apart from cannon fire or exploding gunpowder kegs. They were covered in scratches and puncture wounds. They looked like claw marks. Was that possible? Had body after mutilated body been physically torn limb from limb?

FitzRoy thought Charles had gone mad, of course, until Charles pointed out to him the neat parallel grooves cleaving apart a nearby torso, the claw marks so grievous the dead man's sternum was deeply scratched. There was also no rational explanation for a disembodied head that was lying nearby, a fist-sized puncture hole smashed through its cranium, the empty brain cavity gleaming as though it had been recently licked clean. The facts were mysterious, but indisputable. There had been no war. No mutiny had taken place. These sailors had been attacked, savaged, and from the missing appendages and shredded wounds present on the remaining body parts, partially devoured.

Who could have done such a heinous act? Or perhaps, what? Man, or Beast? Unfortunately, they were about to get their answer.

The creatures suddenly appeared from out of nowhere, bursting out of the shrubbery about thirty feet to their left. Fifteen of them, maybe more, and Charles' blood ran ice cold as he turned and gazed into their black, lifeless eyes for the first time. He was positive this afternoon was a nightmare now, and these strange beasts were all the proof he needed to fully convince himself, for no animal species such as these had ever walked the real world.

His body rooted to the spot by primal fear, Charles' ever-curious scientific mind had escaped the terror long enough to study the monstrous creatures who ignored their presence for the moment, concentrating on finishing the body-scraps they'd left behind earlier.

He wanted to label them as Marine Iguanas, which were plentiful on those islands. They also came close to matching these beasts immense six-foot length, but no species of iguana was carnivorous. The body shape wasn't right either—these animals were far sleeker looking, more snake-like than the bulkier bodied iguanas. The coloring was wrong also—these feasting creatures were slate gray with an off-white throat, whereas the Marine Iguana was green with a fiery orange belly.

If Charles hadn't known better, he'd have said they were large Monitor Lizards. Monitors are meat eaters, but are Old World creatures, indigenous to places like

Australia, New Zealand, and most of Africa. None had ever been documented in the Galapagos area, or even South America for that matter, and certainly none had ever been considered man-eaters.

Then it dawned on Charles, in a moment of perfect clarity before all hell broke loose, that what he was looking at was a completely unknown species. A sort of lizard-iguana hybrid that no other man had ever documented. He'd have been thoroughly fascinated by these ferocious yet stunningly beautiful creatures, had he not been so deathly afraid at that moment.

It was Charles' fear that ultimately saved his life. While he was trying unsuccessfully to categorize the monsters, two of Captain FitzRoy's crewmen made a break for it, screaming in tandem as they tried to scurry back up the steep volcanic ridge. Their high-pitched wails and frantic movement immediately attracted a crowd. Both men were brought down quickly — their agony mercifully cut short. Charles saw only a blur of lightning fast pursuit, a flash of razor sharp teeth, a gnashing of powerful jaws, and then there was nothing left of the men but two crimson splashes on the hot black sand.

A third crewman decided to make a dash for the trees, thinking the creatures were preoccupied tearing his mates to shreds. Two creatures raced after him, catching up to the doomed sailor just as he reached the tree line. He tried to climb his way to safety, but was dragged back down to ground level. Instead of immediately setting into him with their teeth, the nearest beast turned its back to him, arced its long muscular tail high in the air, and brought it crashing down on the back of the struggling man's head, puncturing a four-inch hole in his skull. The sailor twitched for a full minute before lying still, his two killers fighting above him to see which would taste his steaming brains first.

Amid all that turmoil, amid all that death, Charles's mind was spinning — thinking about the smashed turtle shells strewn about the desolate island. He'd been gathering bits and pieces of the puzzle for four years, but standing on that blood-smeared beach, something clicked, and it all started to come together. Not just about these creatures, and how they'd grown bigger, stronger, and savagely carnivorous in a part of the world where nothing like them had ever existed, but it came together regarding all life on the planet. Evolution! Charles finally understood how it really worked, how the most important factor — the key factor — was the environment that a species lived in.

The giant lizard-iguana creatures had developed a hard scorpion-like tail, simply because they'd had to, in order to survive. As meat eaters, and large ones at that, their prime source of food would have been the giant Tortoises. To thrive as a species, they'd had to develop a way to crack through the turtle's thick outer shell to get to the sweet life-giving meat within. If their main source of food had been an animal such as a deer or a goat, they wouldn't have needed the bone-piercing tail. Therefore, it was their environment that had dictated the evolutionary change. Take any other species, establish them in a different environment, and they'd evolve to meet the needs of this new environment — or die off it they weren't strong enough to adapt. Survival of the fittest — it finally made sense!

There was a commotion behind Charles, about two hundred feet out into the bay, but he was too caught up in the moment of his revelation, to notice. Captain FitzRoy snapped him out of his reverie by yanking on his arm, pointing toward the open ocean. Charles turned and saw a large area of water beside the abandoned American ship churning like there'd been a silent explosion beneath the otherwise calm surf. A mammoth beast reared its gargantuan head out of the depths, bearing the same sleek snake-like visage as the carnivores that feasted on the beach, only considerably bigger. Judging by the head and shoulders, this monstrosity must have easily measured twenty feet in length — maybe twenty-five. It began tearing the side of the whaling vessel apart, easily ripping its way into the cargo holds where thousands of pounds of whale meat awaited its ravenous appetite.

A slight inland wind carried the pungent smell of raw mammal to the creatures roaming the black sand beach. As a group — like someone had rang the dinner bell — they all raced for the water to join their huge gluttonous brethren. Within seconds, Charles, Captain FitzRoy, and the one remaining crewman found themselves blessedly alone, forgotten about in the wake of the new discovery of food. They wasted no time, taking advantage of their good fortune and made their escape while they had the chance.

At the top of the volcanic ridge, Charles stopped to take one last look at the grisly charnel scene below on the beach, and at the mysterious unknown creatures thrashing about in the sea. The three survivors quickly made their way back to the Beagle, and made a solemn vow to each other, that they would never talk of what they had just been witness to. Officially, the landing party never found the American sailor's camp, and the three dead crewmen would be reported as missing and presumed drowned. Nothing of that day's events would ever be entered into the ship's log...

***

Lying was easy for them when they were basically on their own, half way around the world — it was living with the truth that became the hard part. The surviving crewman jumped ship at the very next safe harbor, never to be seen or heard from again. Captain FitzRoy would keep his vow of silence, but the strain of the secret may have been a contributing factor in his later decent into depression and his subsequent suicide in 1865. As for my great-great-grandfather, that strange day would forever be engraved in Charles' thoughts, memories, and in his progressively grim dreams.

The unknown species of six feet long lizard-iguana creatures had certainly terrified him, but they weren't the source of his growing obsession. It was the twenty-foot monster gorging in the bay that troubled Charles so. That day on Tower Island had solidified his thoughts and ideas about evolution into what he would call Natural Selection, meaning species evolving naturally according to their environments. Charles also penned the term Unnatural Selection, but he only referred to it in those private journals I spoke of earlier. Unnatural Selection deals with species evolving in an unnatural way — evolutionary change that is a mistake or a freak of nature. The gargantuan lizard-iguana creature would never exist in a perfect world, but as you and I know, this world is far from perfect, and since evolution is happening around us every minute of every day, we're bound to get an unnatural aberration from time to time. Especially now, what with the way scientists are so pretentiously tampering with the genetic code — the very building blocks of life itself.

There are things out there in this huge crazy world, we still don't know about yet. Things being born, things being created, things that have existed for eons, but are only now ready to come out of the shadows to make our sadly unprepared acquaintance. Unnatural Selection doesn't end there either. There are things being manipulated into existence, behind the well-funded closed doors of medical and military research laboratories all around the world.

Even man, as a species, is changing. We're getting bigger, stronger, faster, and intelligent enough that we can now grab a petri-dish and a gene splicer, and take turns playing God. Right now, as we speak, unethical testing is taking place on human subjects, with hideous results. Humans are evolving into things that neither God, nor nature ever intended. And it will get much worse, before it ever gets better.

My great-great-grandfather kept his fears of evolution going haywire, and his dreams of myriad unnatural beasts running rampant throughout the world, hidden. He was scared and had his reputation to consider. I can respect that, but not for a minute do I agree with his stand. I think it was his responsibility — and now mine — to inform the public of all these unnamed, unknown, unpredictable things that are out there, waiting, biding their time until we let our guard down once too often.

This is the reason I've invited you here tonight. I have a proposition for you. Like Charles, I too suffer from terrible dreams about humanity's future, which is why

I've decided to dedicate my life to carrying on my famous ancestor's legacy — scanning the globe for telltale signs that my family's most secret fears are starting to come true. What will I discover on my own dark journey of discovery? To be honest I have absolutely no idea, but I'm hoping you'll come with me, to join the hunt so to speak. What's that? Where will we start? Well, that's the easy part. We'll start where all the best monster stories begin.

We'll find somewhere dark…

Story Notes

This piece of fiction has always been one of my favorites and thought I'd put it here after you've read *All That Glitters...* because that strange species of subterranean golden men are exactly the type of unnatural things our good doctor Darwin will be out searching for out there in the dark. Hopefully he doesn't find them – lol!

I've always loved stories and books where the writer takes real characters and events from history and spins something fantastic or horrific into what actually happened. I've written several historical horror stories like this and I'm currently working on a couple of much longer works in this same vein as well. This tale is actually an introductory story that I wrote for an evolutionary horror anthology I edited called *UNNATURAL SELECTION: A Collection Of Darwinian Nightmares*. I played with the ending a little here, just to give it more closure and feel more like a stand-alone short story but it's a really good collection; one I'm very proud of. You might still be able to find it out there in Ebay and Amazon-land. Someday I'd like to release the ebook of this collection again but the logistics of finding all the authors again and getting them to give me permission to reprint their stories is going to have to wait until I'm a little less busy. I'll work on it, though. Promise.

THE SUICIDE MAN

The alarm clock went off like a neutron bomb, ruthlessly assaulting the sleeping man's nerves, jump starting him instantly awake. It wasn't exactly good for the old ticker and definitely a bad way to start the day.

Simon Taylor rose out of bed only to fall into a deep black pit of depression upon opening his eyes. His first thought wasn't a happy one.

I need to kill myself today. I can't take this anymore. Everything's the same... nothing has changed. Same old crappy bedroom in the same old crappy apartment.

His eyes scanned his surroundings just to be sure. He saw dirty bed sheets dotted with cigarette burns, cheap broken thrift shop furniture on a threadbare blue carpet, faded tacky wallpaper smeared with countless mildew stains running clear up to the crumbling ceiling which threatened to collapse down on him at any moment. No, nothing had changed. Simon was still in the same shithole as yesterday!

A ray of golden sunshine reflected into Simon's eyes, drawing his attention to where it glinted off the surface of the large mirror across the room. It was one of those full-length standup dressing mirrors, all battered and ancient but a tiny seed of hope planted itself in Simon's brain as he gazed over at it.

"Maybe it's *me* that has changed? Maybe today I'll look different?"

He scurried out of bed and raced over to the mirror. His recurring hope, futile as it was, had him metamorphosing overnight into some kind of younger version of Robert Redford complete with bright blue eyes and sparkling white teeth. Hope, once again, died at the mirror.

The silver backed glass revealed a pale, sickly man who looked every second of his fifty-six years, and then some. Statistically, at five foot nine, one hundred and ninety pounds, Simon was fairly close to average proportions but somehow statistics didn't count for a hell of a lot compared to the stark honest reality of a mirror's reflection. He had a small skeletal frame (bird boned, as his father used to constantly tease) and was sadly lacking in the muscle tone department which caused the bulk of his weight — fatty tissue — to appear far more prominently that it should. His fat sagged loosely off his bones in thick jiggling ripples of jaundiced flesh, and the rest of the picture wasn't much better. Simon's arms seemed *way* too long, his legs too stubby, and far more grey hair adorned his shoulders and back than had ever graced the balding crown of his oversized, lumpy cranium. In short, the man in the mirror staring back at Simon wasn't Robert Redford. Not even the older version. Not even close! He looked more like a mountain gorilla than a movie star.

I can't go on like this. I can't pretend things are just miraculously going to get better. They won't. Not ever. I have to die today.

Too disgusted to look himself in the eye any longer, Simon slumped toward the small drab bathroom at the end of the hallway. On his way, he walked past his apartment door, not even glancing down at the growing pile of unread mail and newspapers he was forced to step across. As soon as he entered the bathroom, his eyes were drawn to the little glass shelf screwed to the wall above the toilet. On the shelf his unfolded straight razor waited, smiling at him. It was a thin, gleaming edged smile which seemed to say, *Here I am, Simon… I've been waiting for you, my friend.* Simon smiled back; not even aware that he was doing it. With shaking fingers he gently, almost reverently, picked the razor up.

"You're my ticket out of this scum hole. A couple well placed slices and *whammo*, I'm out of here!"

It felt right to him. Simon could run himself a nice hot bubble bath, climb in to tenderize for a while, then slit both his chubby wrists. Ending things that way seemed almost pleasant. The pain and gore would be kept to a bare minimum and he could just numbly drift out of this rotten world in the warm crimson water. In some ways it was a better death than he felt he deserved but he was far too cowardly of a man to risk anything decidedly nastier.

Simon whistled while the tub filled, happy that he'd finally decided to end his miserable existence. The world would be a far better place without him around to stink it up. The bathtub was half full before Simon realized what song it was that he was whistling. It was an old favorite of his father's, some big band version of "*Some Enchanted Evening*" he'd often whistled along with as he battered his wife and son before, during, and after his many drunken rampages. Simon stopped whistling immediately, shamed into silence by the painful memories flooding into his mind. God how he had hated that psychotic bastard!

It had been Simon's father who started him on this downward spiral toward oblivion. His childhood had been a dark, twisted labyrinth of physical and mental abuse, neglect, loneliness, misery, pain, and constant fear. His mother had loved him as best she could. She'd been just as abused and afraid of his father as Simon had been, in fact probably more. Both his parents had been killed in an apartment fire when Simon was only fourteen years old. In many ways, it had been the best thing that ever happened to him and Simon had always considered it a blessing.

For a few more years things had improved in young Simon's life but not very much. He ended up dropping out of school at sixteen, moving from one dead end job to the next, then quickly falling into a life of crime. It was petty stuff at first; stealing food and cigarettes, picking pockets, breaking and entering, and the odd joyride in a borrowed car.

Petty or not, the judge had sentenced him to two years less a day in the Pen for one of those stolen cars. His first jail sentence soon led to another, and then another, as the road down the strait and narrow became increasingly more difficult to travel. Eventually, Simon had fucked up enough to be given hard time — twelve to fifteen years in maximum security. He'd been thirty-two years old and sunk just about as low as he could possibly go. He'd suffered through some nasty bouts of depression and despair in the next ten years before finally giving up and trying to commit suicide for the very first time. He'd tried to hang himself inside his cell with a bed sheet but the material was too stretchy and all he succeeded in doing was giving himself a mild case of whiplash. There were a few more half-assed attempts at killing himself but Simon's heart wasn't completely into it and he always messed up and failed.

During the psychological counseling that followed, Simon had met the one person who could have possibly straightened his life out forever. Her name was Samantha, the social worker assigned to his case, and she was the most beautiful woman Simon has ever seen. She wasn't perfect, but she was perfect for him. From their very first meeting, Simon knew that he was in love with her. To his astonishment, Samantha started to show signs of affection for him as well. Not right away, of course. It took time and patience but that was okay, Simon had nothing *but* time on his hands.

A few more years rolled by and their relationship seemed to grow stronger. Simon eventually built up the nerve to ask her if he could come see her when his probation was finally granted. Samantha had said, "Sure, I'd love that," and Simon had counted down the days until he was a free man again.

He'd rushed out to buy a brand new suit, some long-stemmed red roses, and a big box of chocolates. A bit old fashioned and lame perhaps but Simon hadn't known any better. By the time he'd rushed over to the address she had given him his heart was ready to explode right out of his chest he was so excited. Samantha was home, in bed with another woman. It turned out that the other woman was Samantha's longtime girlfriend and they'd lived happily together for over eight years. The entire time Simon had been dreaming about her falling in love with him, Samantha had been a lesbian and had only ever considered Simon to be a good friend.

From that point on, depression and self-loathing had kicked Simon around for a while until he'd woken up this morning knowing that today was his last day on earth. The bathtub was full now so Simon shut off the taps, climbed into the hot water's steamy embrace, and lay the straight razor down on his ample belly while he soaked for a few minutes. He came close to dozing off, the warm water lulling him toward the brink of sleep but he shook himself awake before dropping off the edge.

"That's enough laying around, mister," he chided himself. "Time to get this over with."

The razor felt pretty good wrapped in his pudgy hand. It felt clean. Pure. *Righteous* even! In one of those rare moments of perfect crystal clear consciousness Simon knew without a doubt that what he was about to do was the right thing. The *only* thing. Without wanting to wait any longer, he brought the razor over to his left wrist and tried to gauge where best to make his cut. His years in prison had taught him you didn't slice from thumb to pinky like you always see in the movies, but instead you had to cut length ways, from hand to elbow. Would one slice be enough, though? Two? There was only one way to find out so Simon closed his eyes and prepared to dig in.

That's strange, he thought. *Why did I just close my eyes? What am I scared of seeing? I want to die…right? And I'm more than ready to check out of this world…right? So what's the problem?*

Regrets…the answer immediately came to him. Regrets were the problem. The truth of the matter was that Simon really *did* want to die today but he was sad because there were so many things he'd promised himself along the way but for the lack of time or money had never gotten around to. And now he never would.

Or maybe…

An idea blazed across Simon's depressed mind, leaving behind fiery footprints in its wake. He sat up in the tub and craned forward to look down the hall at the pendulum clock on the living room wall, its metal arms pointing to 8:17 a.m.

"It's still early…*really* early. What if I was to get up and do some of these things I'm regretting? I could spend the day fulfilling promises to myself and then by tonight I'd have no more regrets left and I'd be able to die happily. No regrets, man!"

It seemed brilliant. He'd denied himself his entire life up until now so why not live it up today. One special day just for him. If he was finally going to get off this crazy planet, why not celebrate properly — go out with a bang!

Simon excitedly jumped out of the tub and ran to the old desk in the corner of his bedroom, trailing water and soap bubbles with him the whole way. He found a thick pad of writing paper beside the dust-covered telephone and a red fountain pen inside the middle desk drawer.

"I'll make a list, *that's* what I'll do, A list of all the things I want to do today. Doesn't have to be earth-shattering things…just a bunch of *stuff* that I've always wanted to try."

Soaking wet and still butt naked he sat down on the edge of the bed and started writing. Twenty minutes of soul searching later, Simon was finished with his list.

There! he thought. *Now all I have to do is figure out how long each of these things are probably going to take, then make out some sort of a schedule that'll get me back in the tub with the razor before midnight.*

That part of the plan was essential. Simon hated his life and this list wasn't some excuse to let him off the hook and chicken out. It also wasn't some last ditch effort to try enjoying life more either — no way. Simon wanted to die and he wanted to die today. He promised himself he'd finish the list and be back in the tub by midnight. 100% for sure. By 9:25 a.m., time-scheduled and prioritized list prepared, as well as a bag of supplies in hand, Simon was kicking the growing stack of letters and newspapers aside and running out his front door to get this show on the road.

The first few things on his list were simple. A new coffee and bagel shop had opened on his corner about five months ago and Simon had still never managed to find the time or energy to check them out. He happily munched down on a fresh from the oven poppy seed bagel with an inch thick layer of cream cheese, and slurped down two cups of extra strong black java — just the way he loved it. His taxi cab arrived on time (he'd called for it from the coffee shop before sitting down to breakfast) and he had the driver just drive him around the city anywhere the cabby wanted. It was a silly request to add to his list but Simon had always hated how everyone in the world always seemed to be in such a tremendous hurry to get everywhere. He's always secretly wanted to just get inside a cab and relax, to wander aimlessly around town without a care in the world where they were going. The cab driver, an older Irish man with a thick shock of white hair and equally bushy eyebrows kept looking at him like he was crazy, clearly used to people running the great democratic rat race but a fare was a fare so he drove on in silence, content to do as he'd been instructed.

In the backseat, Simon took out his list and scratched off the top two lines:

** BAGEL BREAKFAST **
**CAB RIDE TO NOWHERE **

He smiled and put his list away again. For the next twenty minutes; the exact amount of time he'd allotted for the cab ride, Simon enjoyed the old cabby's confused looks as he pondered which random turns to make. When the time was up Simon tapped the driver on the shoulder and instructed him to head for the park.

Feeding the Robins and Pigeons in the park was the next item on his list and it was a task he relished thoroughly. He'd always thought birds were wonderful creatures, so graceful and beautiful; things that he himself had never been. He'd brought along a dozen slices of stale white bread from home in his little supply bag and spent the next hour sitting on a wooden bench immersed in the wonders of nature.

"This is fabulous!" Simon shouted with glee, startling several of the gathered birds.

For so long he'd caged himself inside his apartment, hiding from the world he hated and only venturing outside when he absolutely had to. He couldn't believe he'd never come to the park and enjoyed himself like this before now. It felt so good to throw caution to the wind and finally let loose for a change.

Throwing caution to the wind was exactly what Simon wanted to do next on his list too. He was planning to have lunch at an authentic Mexican restaurant. He'd always loved spicy foods of all types but Mexican was by far his favorite. Trouble was, he'd had a bad bout of stomach ulcers five years ago and since then he'd been forced to deny himself this small pleasure. Not anymore! Today Simon ordered several of the spiciest dishes he could find on the menu, washing the delicious food down with not one, but two icy cervezas.

"To hell with my ulcers," Simon muttered, grinning like a school boy as he stroked off two more lines from his precious list:

** FEED THE BIRDS **
** SPICY MEXICAN LUNCH **

Feeling better than he had in ages, and still with a little time on his hands, Simon ordered and enjoyed a third cold beer from the bar. Normally he'd never drink this much; especially not this early in the day, but what the hell — today was a special day. Simon's day.

Quarter after one in the afternoon arrived and it was time for him to go into a store and steal something. He'd thought long and hard about whether to put this item on his list or not. He hadn't stolen anything since his latest release from prison years ago but after a great deal of internal debate he'd put it on the list simply to prove to himself that he still had the guts and the judicial system hadn't beaten him down the way it thought it had.

The Gap was the name of the clothing store Simon eventually entered. It was a busy place with loud music blaring out of large speakers built right into the walls. The young sales staff bopped along with the beat, looking bored out of their minds.

Easy pickings... Simon thought, nonchalantly wandering the store while simultaneously keeping an eye on the employees and checking out the merchandise.

Ten minutes later, Simon had himself a nice new navy blue sweatshirt, which was going to come in handy since the afternoon breeze was really picking up and the temperature was steadily dropping. It looked like the rest of the world was in for a long, cold night.

At the nearest bus stop Simon used the glass wall of the shelter to strike off another item on his list:

** STEAL SOMETHING NICE **

Simon folded the paper and put it away in his pocket just as the B-15 bus pulled to a stop right on schedule. Climbing aboard he tipped the driver a dollar and took a seat near the middle of the bus, pleased with the way his day was turning out. The bus was old and noisy but Simon wasn't planning on riding it all the way into the heart of the city. In fact, it only took him another three minutes to fulfill the next item on his list. A tall, bearded man stepped off the bus at the next stop minus his wallet, which was now snuggled deep in Simon's front pocket.

"You can scratch another one off, Simon old boy," he whispered under his breath in case another passenger might be listening. "Haven't lost a step, have you? *Nope*, not a step!"

** TRY PICKPOCKETING AGAIN **

After updating his list, Simon rode the rest of the way in contented silence, excited about the progress he was making and longing to get back to his razor later tonight. So far, things were going great. Perfect, in fact. This was quickly turning into the best day of his whole miserable life.

Simon exited the downtown bus when he spotted a car rental agency on Central Avenue. It was an Avis dealership and Simon had no trouble renting a car using a credit card out of the wallet he'd stolen from the bearded man earlier. By 3:05 p.m. the paperwork was complete and Simon was pulling out of the lot in a Ford Mustang GT. The car was brand spanking new, British racing green, standard transmission, fully loaded, and handled like a dream. He'd always wanted a racy new sports car like this to cruise around the city in but the stagger price had made it impossible. Hell, he couldn't have even afforded the gas to run it, never mind all the other costs associated with owning a vehicle. Money wasn't a problem today though. Today it hadn't cost him a cent.

As soon as he was out of the dealership's view, Simon slammed the accelerator to the floor, testing to see what the Mustang had under the hood. It had a *lot*, rocketing Simon forward like a bullet fired from a gun. For the next hour and a half he tore all over the city, zipping in and out of traffic relishing an exhilarating feeling of reckless abandon.

Joy raced through his veins matching step for step with the raw horsepower of the magnificent engine revving beneath him. Simon rolled down the window and screamed at the top of his lungs, "I hate myself... and I hate this whole *fucking* world," not caring who heard him. God he felt great. Fantastic even! It was as if his decision this morning to finally end it all had somehow released him from decades of bitterness, anxiety, and frustration. He owed it all to his list he'd made, this one glorious day of not caring about anything. Today his only rule was anything goes and to hell with anyone who tried to get in the way. This was *his* day, his one last chance to let it all hang out and finally live life on the edge. He floored the accelerator again and shot off down the boulevard determined to make the most of his opportunity while it lasted.

He pulled over and parked for supper around 6:15, but his south of the border extravagance at lunch, delicious as it had been, caused Simon to bow out of anything too harsh on his already tender tummy. A big steaming bowl of thick chicken noodle soup and a fresh garden salad rounded out his evening meal. Not exactly the classic '*last supper*' by any means, but it was delicious and filling just the same. Besides, he didn't have time to wait in line at some overly busy, swanky five-star restaurant. He had his precious list to complete and time was running short.

** JOYRIDE IN SPORTS CAR **

Simon put away his pen after updating the list, paid his bill, and bolted for the front door. He cruised around town, killing time until 9:15 p.m. when he drove into the older section of the city and eventually pulled the Mustang to the curb and parked on Church Street. This dimly lit street was famous for one reason and one reason only — *girls!* Lots of pretty and not so pretty, scantily clad ladies trolled the sidewalks on both sides of the road here. They were friendly girls, always ready, willing, and able to show a man a good time — for a fair price, of course.

Simon was eyeing up three girls who were strutting

back and forth past his passenger side window, showing of their wares. Simon liked what he was seeing, his heart thumping rapidly within his chest at the prospect of fulfilling the next item on his list.

** SLEEP WITH A HOOKER **

He was still finding it hard to believe that he'd actually scribbled that down on his list but then again, why not? Why feel weird about wanting some company on his last night on earth? He's always been a lonely man who'd lived a hard life; it was perfectly natural for him to want a little female pleasure tonight.

His resolve and confidence strengthened, Simon lowered his passenger side window and waited for one of the girls to stop and approach him. He wasn't all that fussy which of the ladies of the night came to talk to him, and part of him was worried they'd all think he was too ugly and run away. Naturally, that didn't happen, and the girls didn't make him sit and wait long, one of them putting a big fake smile on her face and trotting over to lean in the window.

She was very tall, her legs so long she had to bend at the waist to peer inside. This posture caused her dark curly hair to hang straight down but not down enough to conceal her rather incredibly large breasts from Simon's view. He stared at them unabashedly while the call girl held her pose, pretending she wasn't standing bent over just for this reason. Reluctantly Simon pulled his eyes from her chest and looked up at her face. She had a rather plain face but her eyes were a beautiful shade of dark green. She was pretty, sure, but nothing to write home about. Simon liked that about here though — if she'd been too pretty he might have been too intimidated to see this through. He was nervous enough as it was.

"How you doing tonight, handsome?" she coyly asked, sensing his approval.

"Better now," Simon said, grinning as the dark haired woman climbed into the Mustang's new leather bucket seat beside him. "*Much* better!"

Sex between them was surprisingly good. Simon had been pretty sure he'd botch it up one way or another but amazingly he hadn't. Darla, the name the woman had given him, had taken him to a rundown little hotel conveniently located right around the corner that she obviously frequented often. It wasn't the dirty, seedy place Simon had imagined but it was close. The room had fairly clean sheets on the queen sized bed and that was about the best that could be said about it.

Darla had sensed his nervousness and had quickly taken over things to the point where Simon only needed to hang on tight and enjoy the ride. His pumped up ego thought she *might* even have had an orgasm near the end.

"Yeah, you're a real stud, Simon ol' boy," he said, laughing after Darla had headed for bathroom to take a quick shower.

As soon as he heard the water running, Simon rolled out of bed and removed his list and pen from his pants pocket on the floor. Naked still, he made note of his sexual conquest, feeling incredible for the first time in years. *Decades* maybe. Even better, he realized that he had nearly completed all of the items on his list. There were only two more things written in bold at the bottom of the page, the last of which was obviously about Simon getting back home in time to slit his wrists. That meant there was only one last item to take care of before he could head on home to his fill himself another hot bathtub. One last regret and Simon could finally die in peace. His happy smile froze on his face, then disappeared altogether when his eyes scanned down to the second last item written on the page.

"*No*... it can't be!" Simon whispered, hardly capable of uttering a sound, shocked that it still read the same thing the second time he read it.

** MURDER THE FILTHY SLUT **

How could he have written such a thing? For the life of him, Simon couldn't even remember doing it. What had he been thinking? He must have temporarily lost his mind, gotten caught up somehow in the frenzied preparation of the list and...

"...No," he spoke out loud; probably *too* loud. "That wasn't it at all."

Deep down he knew he'd included it on the list because murder had always been something he'd wondered about. *Fantasized* about. Simon wanted to know what it would be like to kill someone, to stare into their terrified eyes as their life slipped away by his hands. What would it possibly be like? It was a fair question, actually; one a whole lot more '*normal*' people had asked themselves than would care to admit. It was only morality, and of course the fear of getting caught, that kept the majority of people from indulging in their hidden homicidal tendencies. Deep down in nearly everyone's heart, buried within our primal core, the seed of murder existed but usually it remained dormant. It took rejection, suffering, frustration, jealousy, or just plain old hatred to germinate the seed. All that was needed then was the proper window of opportunity and *wham* — another killer was born!

Simon had been rejected. He'd suffered. He'd been frustrated and jealous but most of all, he'd hated. God, how he'd hated! From his abusive father, to his jail keepers, to that lesbian social worker bitch who he'd been stupid enough to try and love.

Simon chewed nervously on his thumbnail as an inner turmoil raged within him. He could acknowledge to himself that deep down he had the *desire* to kill someone but the real question was whether or not he had the *guts* for it. Wanting to kill was a whole different ball game than actually going out and really doing it.

One thing was for sure; Simon was sick and tired of being a coward. He'd been pushed and shoved and backed into more corners in his life than he cared to remember. It was time to stop being scared all the time. After all, wasn't that exactly what this last day of fulfilling regrets was supposed to be about? One last day to live on the edge and do whatever it was that he wanted to.

…And Simon *really* wanted to murder the filthy slut!

He had the straight razor out of his supply bag and into his hand before he could recall making the conscious decision to do so. Staring at the shiny thin blade, Simon was shocked that it had even been in with the rest of his supplies. He couldn't remember packing it this morning but was nonetheless glad that he had. It felt good in his hand. Better than good — *great!* This was the same razor he was going to end his own life with later on tonight; it only seemed fitting to give it a little warm up session — a taste of things to come, so to speak.

Murdering Darla, or whatever her *real* name was,

turned out to be far easier than Simon had believed possible. He simply pushed his doubting conscious aside, confidently stepped into the bathroom, and slit her throat ear to ear from behind as she was toweling off. Several thick arcs of crimson splattered the cheap plastic shower curtain and a virtual river of gore rained down onto the cracked tile floor, but with Darla facing away from him hardly a single drop spilled onto Simon. The woman dropped to the floor at his feet, her body reflexively convulsing, looking quite a bit like she was still trying to dry off, her body not yet aware she was already dead. A few gurgling squeaks and frothy red bubbles continued to burst out of her throat wound but in less than thirty-seconds she lay perfectly still.

Even in death, Simon thought her eyes were still very beautiful.

My god, I've actually done it, Simon thought. *I've killed her!*

After updating his list and getting dressed, Simon watched a little television while wrestling with the torrent of conflicting emotions that were racing through his mind. He felt nauseous and ashamed that he'd robbed a human being of their life but on the other hand he also felt powerful and elated that he'd finally found the guts to follow through with something. He finally decided the positive feelings outweighed the negative. Besides, he didn't have to worry about a guilty conscience haunting him — he wasn't going to live long enough for that.

Thinking about how much time he had left made him curious what time it was. When Simon checked his watch he was stunned to learn it was 11:09 p.m. already. "My god!" he cried in panic, having had no idea it was getting so late. "I have to be home by midnight. I *have* to!"

This had been by far the best day of Simon Taylor's life and he wanted it to be perfect right to the end, exactly as he'd planned. The list was very important to him. It wasn't just a scrap of paper anymore; it had taken on more and more of a spiritual quality as the day had progressed. The thought of not completing the last item in time was something Simon didn't even want to consider. It was completely *unacceptable*.

"Please let me make it home in time," Simon shouted to the heavens as he raced across the hotel parking lot to jump in his rented car. "Don't let me screw this up. Not this time… not tonight!"

He gunned the Mustang's engine for all it was worth, laying twin tracks of black rubber all the way to the first corner. His apartment was clear across the city and even though traffic was lighter than usual at this time of night and he was driving a powerful sports car, he wasn't sure if he could make it in time. It was going to be close; that was for sure.

Simon drove like a man possessed for the next thirty-five minutes, running red lights and swerving around slower cars and trucks whenever he came across them. He ditched the care about a block and a half from his apartment, spotting a parking spot and grabbing it just in case there was nowhere to park on his own block. It was quicker to run than to try and double back. And run he did, literally sprinting for his front steps, moving as fast as his fat, out of shape body could go. When he finally burst into his apartment he was gasping for breath and sweating like a pig. He nearly tripped over the pile of unread mail and newspapers on the floor but somehow managed to stay on his feet. The hands on the large pendulum clock on the living room wall pointed to

11:56.

There might still be enough time.

Renewed hope surged through him, giving his exhausted body the energy to carry on. Simon ran for the bathroom, tossing articles of clothing all over the place in his haste to get undressed. He turned on both water taps full blast and finished removing the rest of his clothes. He had to return to the living room to dig his straight razor out of his supply pack that he'd dropped by the door. He paused an extra few seconds to look once more at his beloved list, which had brought him such unexpected happiness today. The only item not crossed off yet glared at him from the bottom of the page.

** COMMIT SUICIDE **

"I'm going to make it!" Simon grinned, then sprinted for the filling tub.

The bathtub was a bit cooler than he'd hoped and wasn't completely full yet but it was going to have to do. With his razor gripped tightly in his left hand, he used his right to shut off the taps, then started to climb into the tub. Behind him, back out in the living room, the pendulum clock began to rhythmically chime twelve times, signaling the arrival of midnight. Simon's body went as rigid as a stone. Every chime made him cringe, the sound battering into his brain like a merciless physical blow. Even after the clock went silent, Simon couldn't move a muscle; could barely even breathe. He couldn't believe it. He'd failed! Midnight had come, ending the day, and he still hadn't completed the items on his list. He'd simply ran out of time.

"*Noooooo….!*" he screamed, finally collapsing in a heap to the bathroom floor.

Simon lay face down on the tile floor for at least twenty minutes, having neither the strength nor the inclination to get back up. Eventually, he struggled to a sitting position and rested his forehead on the cool rim of the porcelain toilet bowl, feeling utterly dejected.

"I can't believe it. I've ruined everything. All my carefully laid out plans… my wonderful list… all *ruined*."

Tears of shame began to stream down his flushed face and dribble down onto his bloated belly. He tried twice to lift the straight razor to his wrist and end his suffering but he just couldn't do it. Not like this anyway. His suicide was supposed to be the highlight of his day, his crowning achievement to reward himself for completing his list of regrets. His death tonight was going to be a celebration, but now there was nothing to celebrate. Once again Simon had royally screwed up. What else was new? It was just another typical night in his rotten miserable life.

Disgusted with himself and his endless weaknesses, Simon stood up and put his still open straight razor onto the little glass shelf screwed to the wall above his toilet. He was too ashamed to even look at it. Simon let the water out of the tub and stumbled out of the bathroom back to his bed. He was still crying as he crawled into the sack and pulled the dirty covers up to his chin.

"Man, I'm such a loser," he scolded himself. "I can't even manage to commit suicide properly. Oh well… maybe tomorrow things will be better. You never know. I can always hope, I guess."

In less than two minutes Simon was fast asleep.

***

The alarm clock went off like a neutron bomb, ruthlessly assaulting the sleeping man's nerves, jump starting him instantly awake. It wasn't exactly good for the old ticker and definitely a bad way to start the day.

Simon Taylor rose out of bed only to fall into a deep black pit of depression upon opening his eyes. His first thought wasn't a happy one.

I need to kill myself today. I can't take this anymore. Everything's the same… nothing has changed. Same old crappy bedroom in the same old crappy apartment.

He scanned the room for a few minutes, then jumped out of bed to gaze at himself in the antique standup dressing mirror. From there Simon headed for the bathroom and ran himself a nice hot bubble bath and got out his straight razor.

He lay in the tub thinking about regrets for a while, and then instead of slitting his wrists he jumped back out of the tub and ran back out to his desk to get a pad of paper and a red pen.

"I'll make a list," he muttered to himself. "A list of all the things I want to do today. Doesn't have to be earth-shattering things…just a bunch of *stuff* that I've always wanted to try."

By 9:25 a.m., time-scheduled list and bag of supplies in hand, Simon was out the front door and on his way. Once again he hadn't bothered to glance at the pile of mail and newspapers lying in a heap by the apartment door. The newest edition to the ever-growing pile had been slid underneath his front door while he'd been lying in the bathtub earlier.

In large bold lettering at the top of the front page, the headline on this morning's early edition of the *Times* read:

**RAZOR KILLER STRIKES AGAIN!
SIXTH NIGHT IN A ROW...**

Story Notes

Ah yes. Deadlines! You gotta love them. Whether it's someone else trying to impose their will upon us or as in Simon's case in this story, self-imposed, deadlines are a pretty stressful part of all our lives. Sometimes working to a deadline can be a good thing. I know as a writer, I tend to not get my butt in gear and really get down to work until the clock is ticking. It's human nature to procrastinate, I think, and you can sometimes use that ticking clock to motivate you in a positive way. That said, the stress of a deadline hanging over your head isn't always a fun thing to deal with. The anxiety is very real and it can sometimes push people past their limits and things don't turn out pretty.

The Suicide Man is an old, old story of mine. So old, in fact, that I didn't even have an electronic copy of it so I had to retype it all in from an anthology I found down in the basement called BUMP IN THE NIGHT. It was a hand-stapled, 40 page booklet published by a company called Black Petals but there isn't a publication date printed for the anthology inside or out. To be honest, I can't tell you exactly when I wrote it either but it must have been in the early 1990s. Maybe even a touch before that because it was back before there was photo identification on everything. In the story, Simon rents a sports car using a credit card from the wallet he steals on the bus. In my original tale, I had him using the driver's license and credit card from the wallet but had to drop the license off in this version because nowadays he'd never be able to use someone else's ID that easily. I left it just with the credit card and hoped you wouldn't notice — ha!

Anyway, the story still holds up fairly decently after all these years and I wanted it included in this collection because it was my very first published story that appeared in a print magazine. It was my first paying gig too, and if my memory isn't too damaged I believe I was paid the grand sum of $10.00 for it. Trouble was, I think I ordered four or five copies of the anthology at ten bucks a pop too, so I'm sure I lost money on the deal but what the hell. Writers are used to that sort of thing, and at least it meant me still having a couple of copies lying around today so that I could share an early story of mine with you. That's worth more than the thirty or forty bucks that I lost.

To me anyway…

Beneath a Templar Cross

There are no mistakes. The events we bring upon ourselves, no matter how unpleasant,
are necessary in order to learn what we need to learn; whatever steps we take,
They're necessary to reach the places we've chosen to go.

-- Richard Bach, The Bridge Across Forever

June 17, 1870,
 Wittem Castle,
 Maastricht, Netherlands.

Underwater, the blood looks black. Dark stains polluting the already murky tank, dispersing slowly down through the gloom. Coagulating tendrils sink in ribbons, dead fingers reaching for the unmoving body chained to the bottom six feet below.

"How long has he been down there, sir?"

The voice startles Arthur De Muur, focusing on the cupful of elk's blood he's just poured into the tank. He hasn't heard Hendrik, his tall, rake thin young assistant, enter the laboratory. Unfazed, De Muur runs fingers through his wide shock of hair, his thick black mane already sprinkled with a smattering of white despite having only recently turned thirty-two years of age.

"Good. You're back just in time. Coming up on two hours, now. A few minutes shy."

"*Two hours!* Are you serious? Well, of course he's dead by now. *Surely!*"

A smile touches the corner of De Muur's mouth, but there is no humor in it. Obsession, yes, a touch of madness, perhaps, but absolutely no mirth.

"Is he now? The blood, Hendrik. Watch and learn."

The first twitch of the submerged body makes the young man jump and he struggles to regain his composure. He backs away from the tank as the body starts to thrash violently in its would-be watery grave, stretching and straining against the silver chains that securely bind it. De Muur leans in for a closer look. Having expected this reaction, he is calm, far more awed by this inhuman display than fearful. It's the scientist in him.

Hendrik is clearly terrified.

"This is Devil's work. It's impossible!"

"Yes... quite, but I was right, wasn't I?"

"Sir?"

"They can't be drowned. He was just lying on the bottom, biding his time trying to fool us. *Fascinating!*"

The blood in the water stirs the body into a convulsive frenzy for several minutes, its hunger so great it is willing to shred the skin of its wrists and ankles in its desperate struggle to escape, to feed. The chains hold, though, something about the purity of silver robbing the body of its incredible strength more so than the lack of oxygen has. The submerged body eventually bows to reason and settles back into stillness on the stone bottom of the tank.

"What now, Sir?"

Hendrik has found the courage to stand close to his employer again, but still won't approach the tank.

"What else? Drain the tank and try again. Go gather some firewood, lad. Lots of it."

January 03, 1869,
Letter, Arthur De Muur to Sir Duncan Fenton,
High Commander of the Order of Knights Templar.

Greetings, Duncan.

I trust and pray this letter finds you in good health. Another month has gone by and a new year has begun. I'm happy to report I'm feeling much better. Like a whole knew man, in fact. I'm studying hard during my stay here at the abbey — science, anatomy, mathematics, politics, philosophy, and yes, the good book, as you so rightly recommended. It has been three full years now since my unfortunate breakdown, and with your friendship, guidance and kindness, I've seen the folly of my earlier convictions. The preservation and secrecy of the Brotherhood is all that matters to me now and I look forward to the day, with your authority and great wisdom, that I can retake up arms and wear my Templar's cloak with honor once again.

Your servant, and friend,
Arthur

May 12, 1869,
Office of Sir Duncan Fenton,
Rosslyn Chapel, Scotland.

Commander Fenton sets De Muur's letter down on his desk when he hears a quiet knock on his office door. Fenton is a Scotsman by birth, but has spent most of his adult life in France and Belgium, earning his knighthood for a lifetime of foreign diplomacy, representing the crown throughout Europe. Duncan peers at the door for a moment, as if he might be able to see through the sturdy mahogany and discern who stands outside. He takes an educated guess.

"Ferguson?"

"Yes, sir. You asked to see me?"

"Come in William… come in."

William Ferguson is a tall, stocky Englishman with fiery red hair and matching beard. He proudly wears the white mantle of the Templars emblazoned with the red cross over his heart, a uniform still recognizable to all who see it. But unfortunately, due to the greed and stupidity of King Philip IV of France who disbanded and arrested the Order of Knights Templar back in 1307, forcing them into hiding throughout Europe, must now only be worn in secrecy and shadow. William, Sir Duncan's second in command here at Rosslyn, is confident that will not always be the case.

Fenton waits until the burly redhead is seated, then pushes De Muur's letter across the desk.

"I take it you've had a chance to read this, yes?"

"Yes sir, at your request."

"Well… what do you think?"

Ferguson unconsciously rubs his fingers through his thick beard, carefully considering his reply.

"I'm very happy Arthur is doing so well. You know I held him in the highest regard until…"

"As we all did, William," Fenton cuts him off. "But the

past is the past, and as you know, I've been considering De Muur's request for reinstatement in the Order. I'd like your thoughts on that possibility."

For such a large man, Ferguson is looking smaller by the minute, shrinking down into his chair, deflating, clearly uncomfortable with this conversation.

"May I speak frankly, Sir?"

"Of course. Speak your mind, William."

"Very well… I'm against it. Arthur De Muur was a great Templar, perhaps the best I've ever known. Many people, yourself included I think, always assumed he would one day take your position as commander here. But then he… he changed, Duncan. I thought it was just a result of his wife's illness that haunted him, but it was more than that. Much more. He scared the hell out of me when he started telling everyone about those… what did he call them again? *Vaspires?*"

"Vampires, William."

"Yes… *Vampires!* Men and woman who drank human blood! It was crazy talk, sir. De Muur went from being a brilliant scientist and caring physician to a raving lunatic almost overnight. And remember the grail? De Muur even thought these imagined vampires were in possession of the Holy Grail. He had a plan ready to seek each vampire's master out until the head vampire was revealed. Find him, and we'd find the Grail he told me! He stood in full ceremonial dress in this very room and tried to convince the council that these vampires were spreading all over Europe and Britain and that we needed to track down and eliminate them before it was too late? He wanted to restart the bloody crusades, for God's sake!"

"I remember all those things, William. How could I

not? Despite our age difference, he was my best friend... the son I never had. His descent into madness hurt me more than you know."

"Of course, sir. My apologies. I don't mean to sound judgmental... he was my friend too. It's just hard to imagine him back in the brotherhood. The Templar Order is at a pivotal crossroads, sir, and if we ever want reinstated into our rightful position of guardians of the faith, we can't afford to have a loose cannon like De Muur around."

"Agreed. But what if he *has* returned to his senses? Think about it, William. What if he's the Arthur De Muur we both remember from better days? Would he not be the perfect brother to spearhead our legitimacy plans to the Pontiff?"

"Of course he would be. No question. I think the council would all agree with that, but how can we trust him again? I mean... he was caught trying to drive a sharpened stake through the heart of the Spanish ambassador. He'd have been hung for murder if you hadn't stepped in!"

"But I did step in, and the ambassador was fine. If Arthur hadn't agreed to voluntarily live in exile at Mont St. Michel Abbey, I'd have had him locked up on the spot. Arthur was sick though, William. Overworked on the job and heartbroken from his wife's ailment, he simply lost the ability to think rationally and cope with the pressures of the world."

"And now you think he can?"

"Yes. Something in my gut tells me he's ready."

"I don't know. I don't pretend to understand the strange workings of the human brain but to me, once a man is feeble minded, he'll always be feeble minded. If you're convinced he's better I'll go along with your judgment, of course, but we're taking a hell of a risk. If we're wrong it could be a monumental disaster! You understand that, right?"

"I know… and that's why I've decided to see him with my own eyes."

"You're traveling to France? Now?"

"Yes. There's no other way. These monthly letters he sends and the reports from the clerics at the abbey are outstanding news indeed, but until I can meet him face to face, there's just no way I can trust him again. I'll leave you in charge here until my return… with or without our estranged brother."

**June 18, 1870,
Wittem Castle,
Maastricht, Netherlands.**

The flames are already licking at the suspended man's bare feet, the heat severe enough to cause De Muur and Hendrik to take a step away from the growing pyre. Midnight in the castle gardens and everything is quiet other than the occasional snapping and crackling of the timber. The usual nocturnal chatter of birds, bugs, and animals from the nearby fields, conspicuously absent. Even the trees are quiet tonight, no breeze to coax them out of their silence reverie. Everything in the garden seems to be holding its breath, waiting, watching to see what will happen next.

The body on the cross makes no effort to avoid the flames. His clothing starts to ignite. Still wet from the laboratory tank, steam rises into the dark sky like a thick fog from a marshy bog, making it difficult for De Muur to clearly see his captive's face. He backs up several steps to get a better angle, and is momentarily shocked to see the vampire's face. Gone are the rich man's smug, indifferent attitude and handsome aristocratic features. His face is contorted into a beastly grin now, a mouthful of razor sharp teeth and eyes full of pure hatred glowing a faint shade of crimson.

"You're not looking so well, Baron Larouche. Starting to show your true colors, no?"

De Muur smiles, seeing that the Baron almost screams something at him, some insult or empty threat, but manages to control his anger and remain silent.

"Not talking to me tonight, Baron? Oh, I think you will. In fact, I *guarantee* it! You'll tell me the name of your master and where I can find him or I'll make your suffering go on forever. After what your filthy brethren did to my beloved wife, be assured I'm looking forward to it."

The fire begins to consume the chained man, starting with his lower extremities then working steadily up. It isn't until his long dark hair ignites that the demon starts to scream. No human makes a noise like this. It's an awful sound, loud and guttural like a wounded animal in exquisite pain. Within minutes the growing pyre becomes an inferno, the Baron disappearing within the unmerciful cocoon of orange flame, but still he continues to scream. Young Hendrik claps his hands over his ears and turns away, having seen and heard enough, but De Muur watches it all, savoring every second.

The bonfire rages for another hour before devouring the supply of wood and burning itself out. Hendrik and De Muur draw bucket after bucket of water from the stream to cool the glowing embers at the base of the cross but still the oils and fluids from the Baron's charred body continue to hiss and pop like pork fat as they drip onto the hot cinders. The smell of cooked meat is sickening this close to the ruined body, but De Muur refuses to wait any longer to speak to his captive. He leans a ladder against the center beam of the smoldering cross and quickly climbs up so he is face to face with Baron Larouche - what's left of his face, anyway.

A human body would be completely ravaged by the blaze, leaving nothing behind but ashes and bones. This demon is no longer human, obviously, but has still suffered grievous damage. His clothes and hair are gone and his blackened skin is cracked and blistered and burnt so badly that his lips and eyelids have fused to his face. De Muur stares into this nightmare visage and feels no pity or remorse whatsoever.

Removing a carving knife from his trouser pocket, De Muur starts to cut away the charred flesh from around the Baron's eyes. The dead skin flakes away easily as the Baron struggles against his silver chains to keep his eyelids closed. De Muur is in no mood for games and uses the point of the blade to carve the eyelids completely off the Baron's face, leaving him seething with rage and staring wide-eyed into his tormentor's satisfied smile.

"Ah... there you are. Are you ready to talk yet?"

The Baron mumbles something behind his lips but his mouth is sealed shut from the kiss of the flames. De Muur is happy to help him out, slowly drawing his sharp blade across the vampire's cheeks, opening up a raw, ragged wound hiding a set of long white teeth and a lungful of acrid smoke. The Baron savagely snaps at De Muur's fingers, trying to extract a small measure of revenge, but De Muur is too fast for him and easily moves out of range.

"Tell me who your master is, Larouche?"

The Baron is breathing hard, straining at his chains, but remains silent.

"You can't escape me, Baron. I know how powerful you can be, but the cross and the silver will keep you in line. I'm learning all about your kind... your strengths *and* your weaknesses, as I hunt more and more of you down. I know you were once human, like me, but some demon bit you, probably on the neck, and transformed you into the vile creature you are today. I want the name of that creature and you're going to tell me where I can find him."

"*Never!*"

Baron Larouche's voice is an icy hiss, high-pitched and full of venom.

"Oh, but you will. You see that mountain range straight in front of you. You're facing east. The sun will be rising above that ridge in about five hours and I recently learned from a Turkish priest how much you demons love to watch the sunrise. Should be quite a show. I'm looking forward to it."

"Your silly threats mean nothing to me, fool. I know you'll never let me go, whether I tell you or not, so why would I talk knowing the sun will destroy me regardless?"

"The Sun? Oh no, you have it all wrong. The sun isn't your punishment, Baron... it's your *reward*. You tell me the name of your master and I'll let you hang in peace here for a few more hours until the glorious sun comes to put you out of your misery and send you to Hell where you belong. If you refuse, Hendrik and I take you down and back into the castle so we can play with you again tonight. And tomorrow night. And the night after that, if necessary. The choice is yours, demon. Relax. Think on it for a while."

De Muur climbs back down the ladder and casually walks away without another glance back. Hendrik, not wanting to be left alone with the hideously burned man, quickly follows.

**September 20, 1869,
Mont St. Michel Abbey,
North Coast, France.**

Commander Duncan Fenton's journey to the abbey has been rather uneventful. Long and tedious, but as with any trip across the English Channel, arriving in one piece is as good as can be expected. Mont St. Michel Abbey is built on a small rocky island off the North coast of France. The most difficult part of the whole trip is the three-quarters of a mile that separates the island from the mainland. At night, a boat can get there quickly, but navigating the rough coastal waters in the dark is near suicidal. By day, the tide goes out and drops the water level in the narrows to mere inches, making sailing impossible.

Fortunately, there is a naturally forming sandbar providing the only viable option for getting to and from the island. When the tide goes out, a person can walk from shore to shore without ever getting their feet wet, just as long as they are safely onto the island before sunset and the tide returns.

Fenton successfully bridges the sandbar and is soon greeted by Father Pierre Aldonna, the senior cleric of the ten catholic clergymen that live and study here at the abbey. Father Aldonna is a wrinkled old man with thinning white hair and a short scruffy beard. He is thrilled to finally meet Commander Fenton after years of corresponding solely through letters and shows him to his room so Duncan can get some much-needed rest.

Several hours later, after Commander Fenton rests, washes up, and is fed a grand meal thrown in honor of his visit, he finally feels comfortable broaching the subject of meeting De Muur. He's wanted to see Arthur since the moment of his arrival, but didn't want to seem too anxious or in any way not grateful for the clerics hospitality. Father Aldonna understands and is happy to oblige.

"You'll be pleased to know, Duncan, your friend has been feeling wonderful as of late. So much better than when he first arrived here."

"That's great news, Father. I've prayed for him everyday and it does my heart good to know he's feeling himself again. I can't wait to see him!"

"I'm sure he'll be thrilled to see you too. He's always studying in the library at this time of the day. Shall we?"

Together, they head out of the banquet hall and make their way along a long stone walled corridor that eventually opens out into a massive room filled with thousands of leather bound books. Ordinarily, Duncan would have rejoiced spending time in this magnificent library, with it's breathtaking high-domed ceiling and row after row of solid oak bookcases filled to capacity with the world's finest literary and academic treasures. Today, though, his attention is riveted on the dark-haired, clean-shaven man seated at a roll top desk on the far side of the room — the only other man present. The man looks up from his studies, sees who has entered the room and gives a brief, tentative wave of his hand in greeting.

Duncan Fenton stops dead in his tracks, unable to move another step closer.

"What's the matter, commander? I thought you wanted to talk with your friend?"

"I do, father. Very much so… only this man isn't Arthur De Muur."

"What? You must be mistaken. This is the man who showed up at our door three years ago with your letter of introduction. The gentleman with him assured me that…"

"Gentleman? What Gentleman?"

"Tall man, with thick wavy salt and pepper hair. European accent. Nice fellow, now that I think of it. We had tea together before he set off for home. He was accompanying De Muur on your orders, was he not?"

Fenton pieces it all together in an instant, naturally, too heartbroken at the moment to be angry with the man De Muur has hired to live in exile here in his place. Father Aldonna is catching on quickly, but still confused.

"If this man's an imposter… then where in blazes is the real Arthur De Muur?"

"Hunting, I'd imagine."

"*Hunting?* Hunting what?"

"Trust me, father… you don't want to know."

June 18, 1870,
Wittem Castle,
Maastricht, Netherlands.

Dawn approaches, an orange glow creeping steadily westward, an avenging angel to drive the cowardly darkness into hiding for yet another day. It's still dark in the garden, but won't be for long.

De Muur climbs the ladder to visit Baron Larouche again. He has let the demon hang for four and a half hours, alone, save for his thoughts. Time enough for the vampire to have made up his mind to talk or not. Either way, De Muur doesn't care.

Larouche's body is already starting to repair itself, shedding the black destroyed outer flesh on his face, arms, and legs and in the process of growing new sticky pink skin. Remarkably, half of the Baron's severed left eyelid has grown back, but De Muur makes no comment on his captive's appearance. He has more important things to talk about.

"My wife was the picture of health until about five years ago. She was a kind, beautiful woman… much better than a man like me deserved. She waited here while I was running all over Europe, caught up in the futile business of trying to bring the Knights Templar back into prominence. I was such a fool.

"I came as fast as I could once I heard she'd taken ill but there was nothing I could find that was wrong with her. She was anemic and ranting about creatures attacking her in the night. I thought she'd taken leave of her senses and consulted a local doctor I knew in Maastricht named Johan Zubrus. He couldn't find a reason for her poor health either, but he convinced me she needed to stay with him at an asylum he helped run. I hated the idea, but she was obviously delusional and was getting violent whenever I tried to take her outside during the day for a walk or for a breath of fresh air.

"At the asylum, she kept getting worse. I was shattered at the thought I might lose her. One night, when I couldn't stand to be away from her any longer, I rode into the city determined to bring her back home where she belonged. When I walked into her room, I found my good friend Dr. Zubrus bent over my wife with his fangs buried in her neck. She looked up at me from the bed and smiled, and as soon as I saw her pointed teeth I knew she was no longer the woman I loved. My wife was dead to me and all that bastard Zubrus had left me was a monster.

"I ran from the room shaking with anger, fear, and disbelief. I ran away and hid from the world for a whole month, trying to get my mind around what I'd seen that night and what, if anything, I could do about it. Eventually I went back and killed Zubrus but it wasn't easy. I didn't know any of the things I know now. I just got lucky and found him during the day. I chopped his head off with the fire axe hanging on his office wall."

Baron Larouche is somewhat confused as to why De Muur wants to tell him this story but something in his tormentor's eyes has him tasting real fear for the first time in nearly eighty years, since he was turned. Swallowing hard under De Muur's intense gaze, Larouche feels he should say something.

"And your wife?"

"No. She was gone. I'm in the habit of telling people I meet that she's still ill and institutionalized for her own good, but the truth is I have no idea where she is or what horrible things she is doing."

"You can't possibly blame me for this!"

"Yes I can. You… and the rest of the demons like you. You've made me what I am and there's no going back. Now tell me who turned you and where I can find the bastard. Do it now or I promise you'll regret it!"

Baron Larouche is silent, weighing his limited options. The sun is rising higher in the sky, the mountain range to the East fully illuminated now, and the wall of light creeping steadily towards them at the far end of the valley.

De Muur can wait no longer.

"Hand me the axe, Hendrik. We'll take off his arms and legs… make it easier to carry him inside that way."

"*No!* I'll… I'll tell you."

"Speak then, demon. My patience is gone."

Baron Larouche whispers the name of a man and a city. De Muur nods once, contented, then climbs back down the ladder. He is barely to the ground when the first rays of sunlight reach the garden and find their way to the man chained to the cross. For the second time this day, Larouche bursts into flames. His face registers agony, but he is determined not to give De Muur the satisfaction of hearing him scream again. Instead he summons his last strength to shout down to his executioner below.

"May my master rip your lungs out and feast on your heart. I promise there will be no mercy for you."

"Just as there will be none for you… from *my* God!"

March 09, 1870,
Letter, Simon Hesler to Arthur De Muur,
London, England.

I'm afraid I have grave news, my friend. Commander Fenton made a surprise appearance at the abbey last September and our little ruse has been exposed. He was furious with you and angered enough with me that I was thrown into a London prison for impersonating a member of the Templar Order. Former member, I tried to reason, but he was having none of it. Since I hadn't really

committed a crime, he eventually had me released and I thought it best to contact you straight away. I have no idea of the commander's plans, or what he may or may not decide to do with regard to you, but I felt I owed you this letter of warning. Bad days may be ahead, Arthur. I hope I'm not already too late.
Be well,
Simon

June 18, 1870,
Wittem Castle,
Maastricht, Netherlands.

The sun is directly overhead, and without any breeze the heat is nearly unbearable. De Muur puts his back into the tedious shovel work and is soon soaked with sweat. Twenty minutes later the hole beneath the cross is large enough and deep enough to suit his purposes. Time to take what remains of the husk that had recently been Baron Larouche down. He's nothing but bleached white bones, some holding together on the cross, others already heaped on the ground below.

De Muur is half way up the ladder when Hendrik comes running from the castle at top speed. He's out of breath and clearly upset about something by the time he arrives at the foot of the cross.

"Sir… a messenger just delivered this letter for you."

"You read it, Hendrik. I've got to get this demon buried and out of sight."

"I have read it, sir, and you need to read it right now. It's from your friend that used to be at the Abbey."

"What do you mean, *used* to be?"

Hendrik hands him the wrinkled letter.

De Muur quickly reads Simon Hesler's letter and then

tosses it into the hole he's dug in the ground. He remains silent for several minutes, thinking. It's young Hendrik who speaks first.

"Sir? Does Commander Fenton know about Wittem Castle?"

"By that, do you mean will the Templar Knights be showing up at our doorstep?"

Hendrik can only nod.

"Yes, I think they might. Duncan Fenton and I were very close once, and he knows how much I love this castle. He may not show up personally, but I'm sure someone will."

"What do we do then? Obviously we have to leave."

"Not we, Hendrik, me. If they dig up some of the bodies in this garden, I'll be swinging from the gallows soon enough, but no one will blame you. You're just an employee and that's all they need know. You'll stay here and tend to the castle, as always. If I do not return, consider it yours."

"But, you'll need me…"

"Don't argue with me. My soul is already lost but there is hope yet for yours. Whether I like it or not, this is a journey I must take alone."

"But there are Templar Knights throughout Europe aren't there? You can't hide forever. Eventually someone will hear your name and know who you are."

"Not necessarily. Not if Arthur De Muur is waiting here to greet whoever Commander Fenton sends."

Hendrik is more confused than ever, but De muur simply points to the hole in the ground at their feet.

"We erect a marker here, beneath this cross, with my name on it in big letters so it can't be missed. If you're here and Fenton is told I'm dead, there will be no reason to continue looking for me. I'll change my name and carry on as before, only this time I'll kill the vampires where I find them. I've learned more than enough about them now. The time to hunt with a vengeance has arrived."

"What if they dig up the grave, you know... just to be sure?"

"We put Baron Larouche's bones inside. Those teeth will give Fenton something to think about, I'll bet."

Together, they bury Larouche beneath the blackened cross, and begin to make the headstone with De Muur's name on it.

"Go prepare my things, Hendrik. I'll need the stakes, crosses, holy water, garlic, and the silver chains... clothes and toiletries of course, but nothing that isn't absolutely necessary. I must travel as light as possible and making haste is of the utmost importance. I'll finish up here."

"Yes sir, I'll handle it. Just out of curiosity, what will your new name be?"

De Muur considers the question carefully.

"I honestly don't know yet, Hendrik. Larouche told me his master can be found in Amsterdam, so something Dutch, I'd imagine. Van Dyck? Van Buren? Van... who knows? Don't worry... I'll come up with something."

Story Notes

Van... something? Any suggestions? God, I hope you all know who I'm talking about and what his last name is going to be or I haven't really done a good job with this one. Again, this is a story I like a lot. It has that alternate history angle that I love, what with all the Knights Templar and real locations going on. And vampires... can't go too wrong with them. Not the sparkly kind, of course, but when they are mean and nasty I've always enjoyed a good bloodsucker story.

Beneath A Templar Cross was written for a mass market anthology being released by one of the major publishing houses in New York. It was about the fictional character my protagonist will eventually become (and no, I'm still not telling you who he is — figure it out!) and I badly wanted to be in that book. I didn't have an invitation, of course, but it was open to the public to submit so that's what I did. The trouble was I rushed it, the deadline for submissions sneaking up on me and the version of the story I handed in wasn't all that great. I received the rejection that I fully deserved and the book went on to be published without me. I really didn't have anywhere else to try and submit the story to so it sat on my computer going nowhere for a long time. It called to me though, and even though it might be unsellable, I wanted to finish it properly.

So I did.

GENOCIDE

...We wait, in darkness.
A jet-black room, in a jet-black world.
Peter is trembling.
"I hear something. I think they're coming!"
"No Peter," I tell him. "Not yet."
"Yes, they are... I can hear them. They're coming, oh God, they're coming!"
"No Peter," I try again. "It's still early. Too early."
I touch his hand, gently.
He calms down. A little.
Again we wait, in darkness...

Time for us, is quickly running out. You see... Peter and I are condemned to die today — this morning, in fact. Peter is taking it much harder than me, his mind fading in and out like a flickering bulb, but perhaps that's for the best. It will be easier for him to go to his death while swimming in the deep calm sea of insanity. I'm actually quite happy for him. I envy him!

Death will be different for me.

Don't get me wrong. It would give me great pleasure

to join him in that cool void. To swim with him toward the distant shore of our next lives, but I can't. I've come close… believe me, but every time I start running for that frothing surf, something always stops me, pulling me back to shore. My lifeguard or sanity-guard if you will, has a name. Its name is… Anger, or sometimes… Rage, some days even... Hatred! *MY ANGER, MY RAGE, MY HATRED!*

Whatever its name, it prevents me from giving in and quitting. So today I will die, but at least it will be with my head held high and proud. My dignity is at least one thing they can't take from me. Not ever!

But why must I die? And my friend Peter? Poor, sweet Peter, who's never harmed a soul in all of his young life. Why must Peter die? The answers escape me. Haunt me.

You see… neither Peter nor I have any idea as to why we are condemned to die today. We have neither committed nor been formally charged with any crimes. We were never even read our rights. Apparently, we have none. We are simply scheduled for elimination. Peter is almost beyond caring, but I am still very angry. I seethe at the injustice of it all, but there doesn't seem to be anything that I can do about it.

…Except wait, in darkness.

***

…We wait, in semi-darkness.

A sliver of sun peeking over the horizon like a razor slash in the dark throat of night.

Peter is shaking.

"Oh God, they're here. They're here!"

"No Peter," I tell him, "not yet."

"Oh God, Oh GOD, OH GOD….!"
"Easy Peter. Take it easy, it's still too early."
I drape my skinny, bruised arm around him.
He calms down. A little.
Again we wait, in semi-darkness…

If my calculations are correct (they're just thin scratches in our cell floor), Peter and I have been held here for forty-one days. Today is day forty-two. Sadly, for us, it will prove to be a short one, much shorter than the rest of the days have been.

They began torturing us almost immediately upon our arrival. Poor Peter was taken away first. I could hear his screams echoing down the corridor. They went on and on and on. He returned to our cell bleeding, with glazed vacant eyes. It was my turn next.

Only so much agony can be registered in the brain. After the pain tolerance threshold has been crossed and re-crossed too many times, the brain simply blocks it all out. By the end of my first session with their needles and their probes and their electricity, my brain had crawled safely away into a dark quiet place. Thank God for small mercies.

I honestly don't remember much about the subsequent torture sessions. I blocked them out too. They were daily and brutal, that much I recall. Worse for me than the pain, is the knowledge that Peter and I are not alone. There are more of us imprisoned here. A great many more. Cell after cell full.

Most of their eyes are as glazed and vacant as Peter's, but not everyone's. There are a few, like me, who still wonder what the hell is going on. They're just as angry and confused as I am. None of them seem to know why they are here either.

There are rumors, though. Plenty!

In hushed whispers we talk, vigilant bloodshot eyes on guard for the slightest sign of our unmerciful captors. Peter never takes part in these talks anymore. He talks only to himself. The general consensus is that war must have been declared — a war somebody conveniently forgot to tell us about.

Genocide.

That's the word I hear a lot.

"They're going to slaughter our whole race," someone on my left whispers.

An old dry voice, two cells down tells me it is happening in other places as well. This house of pain is only one of many. All across the land, we are being herded up and packed into these slaughterhouses. "Death Camps," the old one calls them. A place to be humiliated, tortured, played with… and then eliminated.

Genocide.

Could it be true?

Could it?

My mind flashes back to the day Peter and I were captured. Our families had been hungry. Starving. Peter and I took to the streets to beg, borrow and steal — anything to make the pain in our young one's bellies subside. At least for a little while.

We were lucky enough to find some food at the rear entrance to an Italian restaurant. It was mostly leftover scraps tossed in the trash, but we did find a tray of untouched pasta that had gone cold and even a fairly fresh loaf of cheese bread. Discarded trash to the rich people whose supper it had been — life to me and Peter's families.

We thought we had found heaven.

What we had found, was a trap!

Stern faced men in dark clothing quickly surrounded us. We fought bravely, but to no avail. That was forty-one days ago.

Why?

God damn it… *WHY?*

The old one with the dry gravely voice says it's because were not like our captors. He says that we're different and they hate us because of it. He also says that they fear us because we are so different from them.

Different? So they have the right to kill us?

Thousands have been eliminated in our captor's fleshy smelling torture rooms and gas chambers since Peter and I arrived. Thousands will probably die after we are gone. They seem to have a scheduled day to die for every one of us. Today is day forty-two. My day - Peter's and mine.

Genocide.

There's nothing that we can do about it.

…Except wait, in semi-darkness.

***

…We wait, in early morning sunlight.

A blinding sun slowly reaching into our cell with a hand we'd rather not shake.

Peter is silent, his mind thankfully gone from this terrible place.

"It's okay Peter," I reassure him anyway. "They're not here yet."

I know it's a lie. I can hear them talking among themselves at the end of the hall.

I hold Peter close, comforting myself probably more than him.

It helps me calm down. A little.

Again we wait, in early morning sunshine…

It's strange the things you think about when you know you're watching the sunrise for the very last time. Of course I've been thinking about my family, they are always first and foremost to me. I hope my beautiful wife Heather is going to be okay. Damn these bastards if they ever lay a finger on her. I pray she carries on without me with her head held high and raises our daughter to be strong and proud of our race. I hope my dear little Samantha isn't too young to remember me. That's not too much to ask, is it?

I pray for Peter's family too, and the rest of the friends and relatives we know. Hopefully, God will spare all of them the fate he has chosen for us.

Maybe God doesn't have any say in it.

Who does then? When I think of our captors it makes me want to scream. One second I want to rip their well fed guts apart, the next I find myself praying for their souls. I hate them for what they are doing, but I'm not capable of hating them the way they seem capable of hating me. Like the old dry voiced prisoner keeps telling me - I'm different. Our race doesn't hate someone without a reason, like they do.

They?

Who are… *THEY?*

That's something I wonder about. I wonder who it was that has ordered me and Peter do die? Who's calling the shots, in other words? What does he look like? How can he possibly go to sleep at night feeling at ease and justified in what he's doing? I'll probably never know. I do know that it isn't one of the big sweaty men around here that are in control. There has to be people above them. Their boss, or perhaps even higher — who knows just how high up the chain of command the orders come from.

In this poor excuse of a degenerating world we live in, the almighty corporate dollar is usually the boss. Those in control of the money are those in control of the power. Some people will step on and destroy anything and anyone that gets in their way of obtaining this power. Once they have it, they'll crush anyone trying to take it away.

It's really sickening, but quite obviously true.

Peter and I are living examples of this modern greed.

Not for long, though. Soon we'll be dead examples!

They're coming for us now. I can hear heavy footsteps rhythmically echoing off the cement floor, like a grandfather clock chiming out the hour.

The hour of our death.

We are removed from our small cell and roughly taken to the torture chamber at the far end of the hall. The sad, haunted eyes of our fellow prisoners follow along with us.

Our executioners are huge muscular men in pale white uniforms. They tower above us like giants as they strap us down on a large blood stained table. Maybe it's just my fear that makes them seem so large. After all, I am very frightened.

One of them notices me trembling and it makes him smile. He simply walks away to help his partner prepare our death. We watch helplessly, as they fill two shockingly large syringes with some unknown amber liquid. There's not much time left for Peter and I. We look into each other's terrified eyes and pray. Besides that, there's nothing left to do.

…Except wait, in early morning sunshine.

***

...I wait, in silence.

A paralyzing fear gripping my heart like a thousand slowly tightening cast iron bands.

Peter is dead.

"They murdered him," my mind screams.

They are going to murder me next.

"No!" I try to convince myself, but I know it's true.

I can clearly see them preparing the next needle for me.

I'm trying to stay calm, but my composure is starting to slip. A little.

Alone I wait, in silence...

How can they be doing this to me? What have I done to deserve being treated like this? So what if I'm different than them, these people aren't God. I have every right to live in peace.

Don't I?

The smaller of the two men slowly walks toward me. He has the long needle in his bloody hand. Poor Peter's blood!

I have time to pray for Peter and hope he's moved onto a better place. A place where there's no more pain... no more hate. I say a quick prayer for myself too.

And then the syringe is viciously jabbed into me.

I feel the tip of it enter me just above the base of my long pink tail. My sharp claws are digging involuntarily into the hard wooden table and the whiskers on my face are beginning to twitch spastically as the poison swiftly courses through my small furry body.

Why is this happening?

Why?

Through a haze I see and hear my two executioners talking above me. I see that it says '*LAB TECHNICIAN*' on the pocket of each of their white coats. They're talking about me… saying something about some big cosmetics company and how they're trying really hard to develop new products for them.

That can't be it!

Please tell me that I'm not dying just so some big company can get rich developing a new shade of lipstick. Please tell me that isn't true! Who gave them the right to decide my life was worth so little?

Maybe if I shout out to them, scream my little heart out, maybe they'll begin to understand. I could let them know that I'm more than just some disposable plaything to experiment with. I could tell them that I have feelings just like them. I get scared, I get lonely, and I get confused!

I wonder if they would even care?

I wonder if anyone cares?

My strength is almost gone now. I'm struggling for just a few more ragged breaths. I know I should at least try to make them understand but it just wouldn't do any good. I'm just a little nameless white rat, and my feeble words would never be enough to put a stop to this madness. The corporate heads of business and science that run this world will always carry more weight then the little defenseless animals like me.

Am I in the middle of a quiet war? Is what they're doing publicly supported genocide? I don't know. I just know that it's wrong. There has to be a better way. There just has to be. Maybe someday, someone will find it.

But that day won't be today.

So I wait, like Peter and the millions of test animals before me, for my death. I should try to talk to them, but I won't. I won't do anything.

...Except wait, in silence.

STORY NOTES

This story is one of my earliest publications. It was published in a long defunct E-zine called *Sinister Element* back around 1999 or so. I set out hoping people would think it was a horror story but then be surprised when I hit them with the twist science fiction ending. At the time I thought I was being quite clever but now that I read it with my more experienced eyes, I should have been a tad more subtle. The tale is a bit heavy handed and preachy, especially at the end, but even with its warts I've always liked it. It marked a significant turning point for me when I realized stories could actually be about something other than just blood and gore and that I could write about things that were important to me. For that reason alone, I wanted it included in this collection.

Memories of a Haunted Man

Toni knelt in front of her son in the foyer and wrapped the scarf around his neck.

"How come we had to come to Canada, mom?" Robert asked as his clumsy mitten-covered hands pulled his woolly hat down over his ears. "Why couldn't we have stayed in Tennessee?"

She understood her son's heartache, but there was no choice. The doctors had only given her father Sam a year, and that was if everything went well. "Honey," she said with a sad smile. Her complexion was white as the snow on the ground outside their Nova Scotia home, and her curly raven hair was the same shade as the sadness she felt about losing her father. "Robby, Mommy had to come take care of Grampa. He's really sick. Can you understand?"

Robby nodded his head. "Yeah, I guess. I suppose it's not all *that* bad here."

"That's the spirit, honey," Toni smiled. "Besides, we're not looking after Grampa all by ourselves. Aunt Pam is gonna help us out."

"That's good. Why isn't Uncle Dave here with Aunt

Pam?"

"Now, Robert, mommy told you we don't want to bother Aunt Pam with that right now. Be glad she's offered to help."

Pam's relationship had gone south years ago, but Dave and her had stayed together for a couple years just to make sure it was dead. Toni's older sister—as dear as she was to her nephew—had a gift for solitude and loneliness. With Dave gone that meant husband number three was no more, and it wasn't that she didn't try. She had always been a loner. As far back as Toni could remember, the only person Pam had ever had a relationship with besides herself was their father. And soon that would be ending.

"Okay, I won't say anything. Promise."

Robby's eyes dropped to the floor, and his chin began to quiver. Sensing his distress, Toni hugged him. "What's wrong, big guy?" she asked gently.

"Is Grampa going to die while I'm at Stan's house?"

She felt her son's pain and shook her head reassuringly. It took everything she had to keep from breaking down herself. She couldn't understand why this was all dragging on, why Robby had to suffer watching his grandfather decay into nothing. "He won't die while you're away, but remember what mommy told you, okay? If Grampa *does* die it won't be sad because he'll be up in heaven. We'll miss him terribly, but he'll be in a far better place."

The boy practically clubbed himself in the face with his mitten as he wiped his tears away.

When Toni walked into the kitchen, she was wiping her puffy tear-stained eyes. "I'm sorry," she said to her sister seated at the table. She was trying hard to keep her mixed emotions in check, part of her wanting to laugh, part ready to burst into sobs. "This whole thing has been so hard on Robby."

"I know," Pam sympathized. "It's been hard on all of us."

Pam had the same black hair as Toni only it was cut in a bob and streaked with a hint of gray. Their father's suffering had marked a turning point in their relationship. The four-year difference in age no longer meant anything, their considerably different lives having been suddenly thrust together. Seeing Toni in such bad shape tore at Pam's heart; she wanted to say something, do anything to help, but she felt numb.

Pam let go of her warm coffee cup and leaned forward onto her arms, wrapped in the warmth of her blue polar fleece. "I was able to rent the house down the street. With Dave out of the picture, I can finally put my attention on dad where it belongs." Pam continued after another sip, "We can take turns watching Robby and caring for dad."

Toni smoothed her hands down her brown sweater and the front of her green pants. Then she sniffled as she walked over to the coffee pot on the counter and poured herself a cup.

"I didn't mean for you to give up your life, too," she said as she sat down. "Dad lived with you for so long after mom died. It's my turn to take care of him."

"We can't look at it that way, Toni." Pam reached out and clutched her sister's hand. The lump in her throat was difficult to speak around. "Besides, I have to do this. He means everything to me…you know that! Daddy sacrificed everything for us when we were growing up.

He and momma didn't even have a honeymoon because he was working two jobs and doing carpentry work on the side just to keep a roof over our heads. How do you repay that?" Tears streamed down her cheeks. "How do you say thanks to a man for giving up his life for you? How do you thank him when he doesn't even know who you are anymore?" She shook her head in regret. "I should have come sooner."

Toni squeezed her sister's hands. "I'm just glad you're here now." She wiped tears from her eyes. "I didn't know mom and dad didn't have a Honeymoon. I knew they'd suffered a lot for having us before they were married, but I didn't realize just *how* much they'd suffered. That's so sad!"

Pam nodded, breaking down as her face fell into her hands. "Family's all you have in the end."

Hearing her father's favorite words brought a wave of sorrow crashing down on Toni, making her feel empty, longing to somehow turn back the hands of time so she could thank her father for everything he's ever done for her. Pam must have been troubled with similar thoughts. "He worked himself half to death so I could waste his money at the University of Kansas and have nothing to show for it." Pam's regret mounted and she bawled like a child. "He never said a word…not one, just told me to hang in there; I'd find my niche someday. God, what a fool I was! I wasted *all* that money, *all* those years, bumming around from one useless man to the next, getting married, getting divorced, getting so depressed I wouldn't leave my bed for two weeks, then starting the same stupid cycle over and over again. I must have been crazy. Hell, I *was* crazy for a while there! I got so damn caught up in my own miserable problems, I forgot all about the only man who ever really loved me for who I was…dad! I'll never forgive myself for that."

Leaning forward awkwardly over the coffee cups on the table, Toni hugged her sister, providing comfort as best she could. Grieving over lost time and regrets had become so difficult for them both.

"You're too hard on yourself, sis. You've always been too hard on yourself. Those battles with depression weren't your fault. You were sick…and you did the right thing by getting some help. No one blames you for that, so give yourself a break. You were there for dad when mom died, right? I'm sure he knows how much you love him."

"What did Dr. Moore have to say?" Pam quickly changed the subject, speaking through tears, not wanting to dredge up any more bad memories.

Pulling away from her sister's lessening embrace, Toni wiped her eyes. "His mental status has declined." She sniffed to clear her nose. "I can even see it here. Half the time he doesn't even know who I am."

"Is he still talking about Grandmother?" Pam was eager for her sister's response.

"It's gotten worse." Toni was uneasy. She didn't like how intently her sister was hanging on her words. "Forget it. I don't want you getting worked up about things we can't change."

"Tell me," Pam insisted.

"He's gone past talking about the abuse. Now he acts out angrily, fights with her." Toni shook her head ruefully. "I think he's reliving all the abuse he suffered."

Pam gritted her teeth. "It makes me sick to think such a good man is left with such horrible memories, all he has left! All because of his goddamn cruel mother!" A strange hardness came to the lonely woman's features—as if one emotion turned off and another turned on. "Do you know what she did to him?"

All Toni could muster was a shake of her head.

"She used to lock him in the closet when he didn't work in the fields as long as his brothers. And how could he, he was smaller than all of them? For a fucking year she made him sleep in the basement just because she didn't think he was worth as much as the other boys. She even beat him when she thought he ate more than his fair share."

Pam drank deeply from her mug then with a voice just barely above a whisper, coldly said, "I wish he would have killed her."

"There's nothing we can do about it, Pam. What's done is done." Toni was afraid of the intensity in her sister's voice, but she didn't say anything. Pam being as close to their father as she was, she sometimes got worked up and a little carried away. Best to simply allow her to let off some steam.

"What about the gun?" Pam asked.

Toni didn't like this line of dark questioning her sister was taking her down, but she answered. "He doesn't threaten suicide anymore, if that's what you mean? His mind is too far gone now. Honestly, I don't think he's capable of thinking it through anymore." She sipped her coffee. "He has no reasoning left, Pam. He's all emotion, nothing but hate for Doris."

"Hell, can you blame him?" Pam asked, seething with anger.

Toni watched the way Pam was grasping her coffee mug - knuckles whitening from her grip, hands literally shaking with rage - and silently wondering if her sister had stopped taking her depression medicine again. It certainly wouldn't be the first time, but now didn't seem like an appropriate time to bring it up. Besides, Pam was a big girl, and could take care of herself, so instead of instigating a potentially embarrassing conflict, Toni decided to just carry on with their talk.

"He picks up the gun," Toni continued shakily, "and screams like he's talking to her about how he wants to kill her and how he's not worthless." Exhausted from the morning's emotional output, her eyes were dry and painful. All Toni could do was let her head flop forward into her hand. "He pulls the trigger dozens of times before he puts the gun down. I usually just leave it in his room. I mean, there are no bullets in the house, and it's the only thing that gives him peace."

Pam stood up. "I'm going to do it, Toni."

"Absolutely not," Toni snapped, "it's insane." She stood up to look her sister in the eyes.

"He's our father," Pam exclaimed, "and the best damn man I've ever known. If it's the last thing I do, I'm going to let him leave this world happy, not stuck in a fuckin' continuous nightmare of dementia!"

"Listen to yourself," Toni pleaded. "This is crazy. I won't let you do it."

Pam responded slowly. Her eyes said it all. She was going to do it. Her father's lessons of loyalty had found a pupil in Pam's heart, and it was family above herself – above all! "Don't stop me, Toni. Money's not a problem, and it's not like I have any kids to worry about. It doesn't matter what happens to me if I do it. At least Dad will finally get the peace he deserves."

Toni sighed. "How can you think like this, Pam?"

"Because I can't stand to see him suffering anymore.

Don't you get it? He deserves better than what fate holds in the cards for him…a hell of a lot better, Toni, and I'm willing to do anything it takes…*anything* to end his suffering! For Christ sakes, he's earned it!" She embraced her sister warmly. "I'm going to do it, whether you support me or not."

Toni knew it was true, all of it. She even agreed with her sister, but the thought of what Pam had in mind was so painful, all she could do was nod her head and weep. The two sisters embraced, searched for, and finally found understanding, or as near as they were ever going to get. Resolve and the certainty of an honorable ending for an honorable man passed silently between them.

God help us! Toni silently prayed.

Toni opened the front door to see Pam wrapped in her down parka, hood thrown up and arms tight around her chest. She shook the snow off her boots, walked into the house. Her skin tingled as the warmth thawed her.

"Mommy, Mommy, are we going to the store with Aunt Pam?"

Toni smiled and knelt to enwrap Robby with a hug, "No honey, just you and I are going today. Aunt Pam has to stay here and…and…" She didn't know what to say. Pam stepped in to help out, but her hastily chosen words chilled Toni right to the bone.

"…And take care of Grampa."

"Oh God, Pam! Why don't we reconsider…" Toni started to say, but Pam knelt down beside her nephew, interrupted her sister's plea.

"What are you and Mommy going to buy, Robby?" she asked the boy.

"A new sled," Robby said, so excited he was bouncing

up and down, pulling on his mother's arm. "Highland Toys has got the new Red Rocket Turbo Racer hanging in the front window. It looks like the fastest sled ever made!"

"Wow, sounds like a beauty. You and your mom better get going then, before someone else buys it first."

Pam pulled Robby in close and hugged him tightly. An internal war waged brutally inside her. Upstairs the man who had sacrificed so that she could have a life lay dying in bed. The time in which she could actually do something for him was fading fast, and in her arms was one of the few treasures she'd ever had in her lonely, messed up life. She hoped Toni realized how lucky she was to have a family of her own. Her eyes brimmed with tears.

"Why are you crying, Aunt Pam?" the young boy asked.

"No reason. One day you'll understand the kind of crazy things grown ups sometimes do, but I hope you never have to make such choices." Pam knew he didn't understand her, but she felt she had to say something. Then the perfect words came to her. "Remember big guy, family is all you have in the end! Now I want you to do what your Mother tells you to, okay?"

"Okay," Robby said.

Toni clapped her hands trying to fake a good mood. "Head on out to the car, Sweetie. I'll be right there." After he thunderously stomped his way out the house, the sisters were alone.

Pam hugged Toni firmly. "Thanks, kid. Don't worry about anything. Everything is going to be just fine."

"Are you sure?" Toni asked.

"Positive. Get going."

Toni kissed her sister on the cheek and hurried out the door before she completely lost her nerve and broke down sobbing.

Pam looked at herself in the bathroom mirror, rage burning within her as she thought about her grandmother Doris. It was because of her that her father was tortured in these final weeks of his life. Doris Petigo was in hell screaming steadily if a God existed, and the satisfaction of justice brought a smile to Pam's face.

Withdrawing the revolver from her dress pocket, she looked in the cylinder: six bullets. She tucked the pistol back in her pocket and hurried down the hall to the closed bedroom door. Without a sound, she pushed it open. She crept to the nightstand, the gun held only inches away from her beloved father's temple as he slept on, oblivious to his daughter's presence. Pam could have ended his suffering right then and there, just pulled the trigger and been done with it, but if she did he'd die without ever knowing the happiness and contentment she'd vowed to give to him. Instead, Pam took a deep breath to steel her nerves, and placed the gun down on the nightstand within her father's reach.

"Wake up you lazy bastard!" she shouted.

Sam opened his eyes, looked up. Fear clutched his heart. "Oh God…it's you! I'm not lazy, mom," Sam said. "I'm just resting from all the work I've done in the field." Her cold eyes drilled into him. "I'll be back at it after supper…promise."

Underneath, Pam's heart was breaking, but she reached out and slapped him. "Good for nothing waste," Pam's voice quivered and tears stained her cheeks, "I wish you would have died at birth!" Even though merely part of the act, her words stung her to the soul.

"I'm sorry, mom." Sam sat up. "I'll do better."

Why wasn't he getting angry? Pam didn't know how long she could keep the facade up. She had had no inkling of an understanding of just how difficult it would be to carry this off.

Sam started to weep. "I wish I could do better, but I'm just a bad boy."

No Dad! she thought, *you're not bad, don't you understand! We love you, everything you ever did was for us. Do it, daddy, please. I want you to have this. I want to give you a billionth of what you've given Toni and me.*

Sam began to breathe heavily. "I try Goddamn it! I always try my best, but you're never satisfied!"

That's it dad...get angry!

"My whole life you've treated me like dirt, momma, and it's not fair. Not fair, I tell you! Who the hell are you to call me worthless? I hate you! I've always hated you!" Sam screamed, shaking with rage.

All of a sudden, the whole thing seemed cruel, but Pam forced herself to continue. It was now or never. There was no way she could go through all this again.

Her hand reached out, and she slapped him even harder across the face. "Good…'cause I hate you too, you good for nothing loser!" She began to bawl, makeup running down her face on the flood of tears. "I'm gonna lock you back in the closet, Sammy! Lock you in there for a week!"

Gritting his teeth, pushed beyond his breaking point, Sam reached for the nightstand. He picked up the revolver, a murderous smile beginning to form on his lips. "The hell you will! I should have done this long ago!"

He pointed the gun at Pam's chest and pulled the trigger. Again and again, his finger twitched on the trigger repeatedly, violent explosions echoing through the room.

Sam was still pulling the trigger of the long-emptied gun, when Toni came home an hour later, a huge contented smile plastered on his tired, ancient face.

"Dad? What are you doing still…I mean, where's Pam?" Then Toni saw her sister sprawled out on the floor on the far side of the bed, bullet holes and blood everywhere she looked. But something didn't fit, old-fashioned blue dress, hair dyed brown and cut shorter.

An awful dread clutched Toni's heart like the hand of death placed gently on her shoulder in a dark and lonely room. In the eyes of a demented man rapidly loosing reason, she must have looked just like Doris Petigo. "Noooooooooooo!" Toni screamed, realizing what it was her sister had done. "Why Pam…why?"

The world turned upside down then, darkness descending, and Toni fell to the floor unconscious. Sam just kept right on pulling the trigger and smiling, happier now than he'd been in his whole life.

Click! Click! Click!

Story Notes

Memories can be funny things. We have good ones and we have bad ones, and over the years the cruel hand of time starts to chip away at us and we'll start to forget a lot of them. Not all of them, though. No, we'll retain the ones that are important to us, or the ones that affected us the most as we lived our lives. Unfortunately that means we sometimes get to keep and relive the bad memories along with all the happy ones. Alzheimer's disease is prevalent in our society and all you have to do is take a walk through any long term care facility or old age home to see how savagely the loss of memories can destroy our elders. Perhaps forgetting isn't always a bad thing though. Perhaps there are some people out there who wished they could forget some of the terrible things that have happened to them in their lives. It's not that easy though, and that's the gist of the story you just read.

Memories of a Haunted Man is a collaboration I did years ago with a good friend of mine named Everette Bell. Everette lives in Kentucky and him and I have never actually met in person but we've spent countless hours together online first as fiction editors at a defunct webzine called Sinister Element, then later as co-writers of four or five decent movie scripts that still haven't seen the light of day.

Memories almost suffered a similar fate. We wrote it and had it accepted for a small press horror anthology called Terrible Beauty, Fearful Symmetry, but the publisher went belly up just as the book was going to print and I doubt anyone other than the contributing authors and editors ever actually saw it. Everette and I even sold the movie rights to this story once upon a time to a guy who was putting together a trilogy-of-terror type film, of which our story was going to make up one of the sections. We even got paid for that film option but unfortunately that was the last we ever heard from the filmmaker and to my knowledge the movie was never made. Regardless, it's a good story dealing with a highly dysfunctional family and how time and the heavy burden of their memories can ravage the elderly people we love and care for. I'm happy to finally have more people finally get a chance to read it. If you enjoy the story, please take the time to check out more of Everette's excellent work. You can look him up and buy more of his fiction here:

www.wartoothebooks.blogspot.com

LOST IN A FIELD OF PAPER FLOWERS

Whenever evil befalls us, we ought to ask ourselves, after the first suffering,
how we can turn it into good? So shall we take occasion, from one bitter root, to raise perhaps many flowers.
-- Leigh Hunt (1784 - 1859)

A teenage boy lies in a coma.

Fell down the stairs, bumped his head.

Ask his father, standing by his bedside. He's telling everyone that's what happened.

Don't ask the poor boy's mother, though. No, not her, she's far too busy crying.

***

Existence #1: Dreamland
"Hello?"
"Can anyone hear me?"
There's fear in your voice. No panic, yet, but definitely

a hint of alarm. At first this strange dream had been thrilling, running and playing in this massive field of orange-red dirt; something you'd never have been able to do from the seat of the wheelchair in real life. The euphoric freedom of standing, of actually *running* on your own two legs is a joy you'd nearly forgotten. Two years have passed since the accident left your spine twisted, legs withered and useless. But in the dream you're running full out, pumping arms, chasing your shadow across the unusual colored soil with the exuberance and energy of youth. It feels great to be healthy again, to be *whole*.

It isn't until your feet slip, and you roll laughing to a stop in a swirling cloud of dust that you begin to wonder about your surroundings. What kind of field is this, anyway? A farmer's field, by the looks of it, the soil cared for and plowed in even, parallel grooves. But if this is a farm, where are the barn, crops, animals, or the farmer for that matter. Standing up, you slowly turn round, trying to spot something familiar. Surely there's a fence line, a pond, or a nearby road. There's nothing, just an endless expanse of flat, orange-red dirt for as far as the eye can see.

You strain to hear any of the normal everyday sounds like birds, airplanes, insects, wind, laughter, but this field is void of those things — a dead place that despite its vastness begins to close in on you, the dusty air tickling your throat, making you dry swallow your first taste of fear.

"Is anyone out there?"

"Where am I? Please…somebody answer me!"

Inside your head you hear a woman's voice, tiny and faint, as if spoken across a great distance. You can't make out the words.

"Momma?" you ask, confused.

No, boy, I'm not your mother. I'm a friend.

"A friend? What do you want?"

To help you get back home.

"I don't know what you mean. Where are you?"

A long way off, but closer than you think. Don't worry about it right now. Stick out your right arm, then turn and walk in that direction. I brought you something.

You're more confused than ever, but at least you aren't feeling as scared. Even a phantom voice is welcome in this desolate place, better than being alone. You do as instructed, and are soon walking in a new direction. You walk for ten minutes, not at all sure why you're doing this.

"Where am I supposed to be going?" you finally ask, but there's no reply. "Hello? Are you still there?"

Silence, inside and out.

You stop, unsure what to do next, considering retracing your steps--

Something green stands out in the orange-red distance.

"What's that? Is this what you brought me?"

A whisper: *Yes.*

You start running, excitement and curiosity propelling you toward the small green dot on the horizon. Slowing your pace, you walk the final thirty feet. It's a flower! A light green carnation growing out of the otherwise barren soil. Its stem reaches up past your knees, its flower round, symmetrical, and in full bloom. Beautiful, sure, but it looks so strange and out of place growing on its own in this massive field. You don't know what to make of it.

"You brought me a flower? Why?"
Silence.

Existence #2: Reality

"Stay cool, Sally. I told you ten times already, I got it covered. You don't need to say squat to anyone."

The tall man spoke quietly, checking over his shoulder down the corridor as he led his wife firmly by the arm into their son's private room.

"But, Paul, I'm just—"

"But nothin', Sally. Let me do the talking and everything will be fine. Understand?"

Sally nodded her head, but Paul wasn't looking at her anymore. She followed his gaze over to the foot of their son's bed, where a small woman stood leaning on a wooden cane. Even before the woman turned to face them, it was clear she was old and obviously quite frail. Her left eye was completely white, no iris or pupil, her vision clouded by a thick milky cataract. When she lifted the corners of her mouth to smile, it seemed to take a Herculean effort, depleting her limited energy. Sally felt pity for the poor woman.

"Who are you?" Paul asked, his tone confrontational. "What are you doing in Robbie's room? This is a private suite."

"Is it? Forgive me, Mr. Moore. I just came to see how Robbie was doing and bring him a little flower to cheer up the room. I meant no harm."

Sally pulled her eyes away from the diminutive woman to look at the blossom laying at her son's feet on the bedspread and noticed that it wasn't a real flower, but rather a paper one intricately folded using several layers of thin green onion paper.

Paul, not even noticing the flower, continued on. "You a nurse or something?"

This caused the old woman to smile, her face lighting up and revealing some of the beauty she'd possessed in her youth.

"Good Lord, at *my* age, I sure hope not!"

"Who are you, then?" Sally asked gently, trying to diffuse her husband's anger.

"The doctors and nurses all call me Aggie."

"Yeah, well, nice to meet you, but my wife and I would appreciate it if—"

"Did you make that flower, Aggie?" Sally interrupted.

"Why yes, I did." Aggie said. "It's called Origami. Learned how in craft class down on the ground floor."

"The assisted living center?" Sally asked.

"Yep. That's where I live, you know? Been there… well, seems like forever."

"Then maybe you'd best get back," Paul said sharply. "Robbie needs rest and I'm sure the nurses will be wondering where you are."

"Heavens! You're probably right," Aggie nodded and started shuffling toward the door, leaning heavily on her cane for support. "Can I come for another visit tomorrow? Don't like to brag, but everyone says I have a special way with children. Maybe I can help?"

Paul was about to object, but Sally beat him to the punch. "Yes you can, Aggie. Just make sure the people on your floor know where you are, okay?"

"Sure will. Thanks."

Halfway out the door, Aggie stopped. "Hospitals are strange places. Buildings made of concrete, glass, brick, and steel; built strong enough to withstand years of pounding from wind and rain, but they're helpless to contain the surge of pain and suffering emanating daily within their walls. All that suffering…it has to go somewhere, don't you think?"

The tiny old woman left without another word, leaving Paul and Sally staring after her in stunned silence.

"What was that all about?" Sally asked.

"Nothin' Sally, just a crazy old fool who likes to hear herself talk. Probably out of her freakin' mind, and you're gonna let her visit Robbie."

"She's harmless."

"I don't care. Tell the nurses that Robbie has no other visitors, especially nutty old bats from downstairs!"

Existence #1: Dreamland

"Are you still there?"

You wait a long time for the phantom voice to answer, standing ramrod straight, eyes closed, ears open, hoping the woman will talk and not leave you alone in this bleak place. Well, you aren't completely alone. You have the flower.

Feeling frustrated and lonely, you sit down in the dirt to study the green flower closer. It looks like a normal, everyday carnation, only slightly bigger. Leaning in close, your nose almost touches the delicate petals. You inhale deeply, and again, savoring the sweet fragrance. It smells wonderful, reminding you of your mother and the small garden she lovingly tends in the yard back home.

Back home--

You shut that thought off immediately, not willing, or able to go down that dark road just yet. A single tear runs down your cheek, a tiny drop of loneliness that escapes the raging river of self-pity building steadily within you.

Time & Space

The tear curls around your lip, dangles from your chin, then drops silently into the center of the carnation.

The flower begins to grow.

Jumping to your feet, you watch in awe as the flower expands, the stalk as well as the bloom growing in front of your eyes. The story of Jack and the Beanstalk pops into your head, and for a moment you think this is how the mysterious woman plans on helping. Unfortunately, before you can envision the carnation growing up through the clouds and climbing it to find your way back to your family, the flower stops growing, leveling off just under the height of your chin, the bloom a full eight inches in diameter. A huge flower, the biggest you've ever seen, but still no help as far as you can see.

Disappointed and angry, you reach to rip the mutant flower out of the ground. You grip your right hand around the thick stalk and...

...you're looking down upon yourself. Not here and now. Has to be several years back. You're younger, smaller, dressed in a blue baseball uniform; knee-high socks, cap, and glove. You are hot and sweaty, the uniform stained with dirt, a huge contented grin on your face—

You shudder, realizing there is no wheelchair...yet.

Your father's shiny new Mazda RX-7 roars into the scene, skidding to a stop in a shower of dust and gravel. From above, you can easily see how drunk he is as he climbs out of the car and starts waving for you to hurry up and get in. Back then you hadn't been able to tell, hadn't had a clue your father had taken the afternoon off work to tie one on with a few buddies down at the local pool hall. Now, you know better. Horrified, you watch yourself climb into the car fully trusting your father to take care of you and get you home safely.

It wasn't going to happen.

You watch the Mazda squeal out of sight, knowing that three intersections away your father will run a red light and a yellow Ryder rental truck will t-bone the car on the passenger side, tearing the small foreign car nearly in half, ending your baseball playing days forever...

The strange vision fades slowly from sight, water down a semi-clogged drain, and you are staring at the green flower gripped in your closed fist. Your hand is sore, fingers cramping, so you let go of the carnation, only then noticing the thin ribbon of blood running the length of your palm, dripping steadily onto the parched dirt below. Seeing the blood triggers pain, and your hand begins to burn. Examining the hand closer, it doesn't appear to be much of a wound, hardly a scratch in fact, more like a superficial paper cut, but it hurts badly and bleeds as if it were a gash cutting right to the bone. You reach for the flower again, to carefully check for hidden thorns on the stem. Your finger has barely caressed the smooth stalk when you wince in pain and pull your hand back to find yet another paper-thin cut. Blood runs freely from both wounds now, and no matter how hard you think about it, you can't understand why touching the flower is cutting you. It's as if the flower is coated with invisible razor blades.

Trying not to panic, you remove your t-shirt and are about to wrap up your injured hand when something incredible happens. The bleeding stops all on its own. The thin wounds begin to heal, the torn skin re-knitting back together as the pain fades away. Within seconds, your right hand is fully healed and the only sign that you've ever been bleeding are the scattered crimson stains on the ground at your feet.

You don't understand what has just happened; don't understand any of this, in fact. Where are you and why is all this crazy stuff happening? The only certainty right now is that you desperately want to go home.

But for seemingly hours you roam the barren field, at times calling out for the phantom woman to speak again, sulking around depressed and afraid you'll be left here in this awful place forever. No matter how far you walk, or which direction you choose to step, you never allow yourself to lose sight of the green carnation — your anchor in this wasteland.

The sky begins to darken. Spending the night in this field, alone in the dark, is a terrifying prospect, but staying near the mysterious flower gives you some comfort, some sense of protection, even if it's only in your head. You lie down on the ground and curl around the base of the giant carnation, and soon fall fast asleep, totally oblivious to the fact that all around you the field is coming alive and the flowers are finally starting to grow.

Existence #2: Reality

Paul and Sally Moore made it home from the hospital in record time. Paul had bitched about the downtown traffic regardless of their progress but that was just the way he was and Sally was used to it. Climbing out of the car, she stood by the front door of their Cape Cod home, waiting for Paul to unlock the door. For some reason, he was still sitting in the car. When she went back to check why, Sally saw Paul trying to wipe tears from his obviously red-rimmed eyes.

"Why are you crying?" Sally asked.

"I'm not," Paul shot back defensively. "I'm just, you

know, upset about Robbie. He looked so small in that bed. So...*fragile*. Is he gonna die, Sally?"

Tears filled Sally's eyes too, thrilled and a little shocked at her husband's unexpected show of emotion.

"I don't know, honey," she said. "The doctor said it could go either way. Come on in, let's have a nice supper and we can talk about it, okay?"

When he finally came up the stairs onto the porch she noticed a red stain on the collar of his shirt.

"Jesus, you're bleeding, Paul. What happened?"

"Where?" Paul asked, looking at both his hands and then down at the rest of his body. "I don't see anything."

"Your neck. Come here. You must have scratched yourself."

Paul looked down at his hands again, saw there was no blood under any of his nails, but shrugged and let his wife take care of him.

Sally took a Kleenex tissue out of her purse and began cleaning up the mess. Fortunately, there were only two small wounds, one long thin cut and one nothing more than a scratch, neither very deep. As she dabbed at the cuts, a tiny brown spider dropped onto the shoulder of Paul's shirt, startling her and making her pull back her hand.

"What's the matter?" Paul asked.

"Nothing. Just a little spider on your—"

"*Where?*" Paul cried, beating his hands all over his head, chest and back.

Sally knew about her husband's lifelong fear of spiders. "Relax, Paul, it's long gone," she said, trying to calm him.

Sally returned to checking his cuts, but Paul pushed her hands away and stomped off into the house. Two band-aid's later, the matter was forgotten, and Sally went to fix Paul's dinner. He wasn't the kind of guy that liked to be kept waiting, especially after his little freak-out on the porch. He'd be mad at himself, feeling silly, and Sally knew from experience he'd be looking for any opportunity to prove what a *real* man he was.

Back at the hospital, Aggie had spent the rest of the day in her room, refusing to even eat dinner. She was busy making flowers, dozens of them, her knotted old hands twisting and folding the thin colorful paper hour after hour, carnation after carnation, until the nurses came to shut off her light and gently force her into bed.

Her body was exhausted and she quickly fell into a deep but troubled sleep. Aggie dreamed about a horrible car accident and of a young boy dressed in a blood-drenched baseball uniform trapped and screaming within the wreckage. The dream played over and over, the boy's pain-filled screams haunting her throughout the long night.

When she finally woke, covered in a fine sheen of sweat, the digital clock beside her bed read 4:58 a.m. The sun wouldn't be up for at least another hour but Aggie didn't care. She couldn't stay in bed another minute. She swung her feeble legs down onto the floor, using her wooden cane to climb shakily to her feet. Middle of the night or not, there was work to be done.

Existence #1: Dreamland
Wake up.
You stir, hearing the voice but ignoring it.
Come on; time to open your eyes.
This time you recognize the woman's voice and bolt to

your feet, your heart trip-hammering inside of your chest.

"You came—"

Your words are lost as you open your eyes to something truly amazing. There are flowers *everywhere!* An entire field, no an entire *world* filled with huge, carnations--a kaleidoscope of color spreading out from the small circular clearing you've slept in for as far as your eyes can see. It's an incredible sight, literally taking your breath away.

Are you with me?

"Yeah, I'm here. Where did all these flowers come from? Did you bring them?"

You hear chuckling.

Heavens, no! Some of them, sure, but I think your mind did a lot of this planting on its own. That's good; it means you're ready.

"Ready for what?"

Ready to come home, of course.

"But how?" you ask. "I don't even know where I am, never mind how to get home! What good is a field of flowers for finding—"

Run, boy, the voice interrupts. *Trust me. Trust yourself!*

You look out across the endless expanse of flowers, not sure what to do. Then you remember what happened last night when you touched the original green carnation. Twice you'd come into contact with the flower and both times it cut you open and made you bleed. Would these flowers hurt you as well?

Run!

"I can't!" you cry back. "I'm scared. They're going to cut me, just like before. Please, I don't want to hurt anymore!"

I don't want you to hurt anymore either. That's why I'm here to help you.

"How?" you ask, frightened. "How can you stop the flowers from cutting me?"

There's a pause, then: *I can't. The flowers are made of paper…and they will cut you. They'll cut you bad!*

"Then why would you want me to run? Who are—"

Shhhhhhhhh, listen. Think about what happened to your cuts?

"They healed."

No. They didn't heal; they just went somewhere else.

"I don't understand."

In the real world, pain has to be suffered by those who receive it. Not here. Here, pain can open doorways all on its own, and can be shared by those who truly deserve it.

"My father?" you hesitantly ask, a tiny flame of hope igniting within you.

Silence.

Tears start running freely down your face. You let them come this time, let your pent up river flood out in twin torrents.

"I hate him. Always have. And not just because of the car accident. Not just because of my legs. He…he still hurts me. Me and momma both."

You break down completely, sobbing into your hands for several minutes, but not for a moment are you ashamed of your tears. No, the tears give you strength, give you courage; help wash away the wall of fear your abusive father has built within you.

And this last time?

"I was listening to my stereo up in my room. I didn't know he was trying to sleep, didn't even know he was home. He came upstairs and he was so damn mad. I tried to say I was sorry…tried to explain, but he had this insane look on his face. He smashed my radio against the wall then grabbed my wheelchair and shoved me out into the hall over to the stairs. Then he...he--"

I know what he did, boy, knew as soon as they brought you in. Bottom line is you don't deserve to suffer anymore. Neither does your mother. That's why I want you to run, Robbie. It's going to hurt, but you need to run anyway.

Your tears are gone now. So is your fear. Your mind made up.

"Bastard!" you yell, and with just that one word you're gone in a flash, running like you have winged feet.

The flowers make you bleed with every step, the stems, leaves, and pretty colored blooms slicing and ripping open your tender flesh as easily as barbed wire. Not all the carnations have grown to the same height, some tear at your knees, others at your thighs, hips, throat, ankles, chest, and face. It's like being attacked by a nest of angry hornets, with no way to avoid their single-minded fury. The pain is excruciating, a monstrous all-consuming inferno, and you run open-mouthed, screaming in agony but it doesn't slow you down. Your clothes are tattered and shredded, your momentum flaying the crimson-soaked rags free of your body, taking away strips of your skin too, but still you run on. Nothing can stop you now.

The blood drains down your forehead, stinging your eyes like pepper spray, threatening to blind you, to force you to stop, but it's through this red-blurred vision of the field that you finally spot the door. It's just a dance of light in the shape of a doorframe, a slight shimmer of motion like the heat haze coming off the road on a hot summer day, but you recognize it for what it is. You lower your head, pump your arms, and run flat out fully aware you're likely using your legs for the very last time. You don't care. All you want is one simple thing: to go home.

Existence #2: Reality

Sally would have preferred to skip breakfast and head straight to the hospital, but she knew better than to suggest such a thing. Paul would hit the roof. No, it was better to just put on some coffee, scramble a few eggs, and keep the peace. The sooner her husband ate, the sooner she could go visit Robbie again.

"Your eggs are ready, Hon!" she shouted from the foot of the stairs, knowing Paul was up in the bathroom shaving. "Best eat them while they're hot!"

It was as close as she dared telling him to hurry up.

Paul responded with a series of escalating screams.

Before Sally could react, her husband appeared at the top of the stairs, naked, his body bathed in blood. He was still screaming, his eyes tightly closed, his crimson-streaked arms flailing around in panic. Sally screamed too, grabbing the banister for support, her legs threatening to collapse out from under her. From where she stood, she couldn't see the myriad cuts on her husband's ravaged body, but she didn't need to for her to understand how grievous Paul's injuries were. She nearly went to him but hesitated, instinctively knowing her husband was already beyond help.

Paul stumbled; rolling head over heels down the staircase, blood splashing everywhere. Sally backed up out of the way, but Paul's progression, as well as his screams came to a sudden, sickening stop when his head connected with a brutal *thud* on the thick newel post at the bottom of the staircase.

Sally couldn't bring herself to take a close look at her husband's body, much less touch him to see if he might be okay. Instead, she took a moment to compose herself, then went to the phone and dialed 911. By the time the paramedics arrived, Paul was still alive, but in critical condition with a massive dent in his forehead where he'd struck the post. There were no cuts visible on his body and not a trace of blood anywhere in the house.

At the hospital, Robbie woke up gasping for breath, fragments of a bad dream lingering in his sleepy thoughts. He was covered in sweat, and was so tired he felt like he'd just run a—

Run! The echo of a familiar voice drummed in his head.

His eyes snapped open, a collision of thoughts, sensations, and vivid memories invading his consciousness, remembering everything at once.

Robbie immediately noticed the old woman standing at the foot of his bed, but then his eyes moved down to take in the colorful paper flowers strewn on the bed at his feet. Peripherally, he could see his wheelchair leaning against the far wall, but instead of looking at that old enemy, his eyes were drawn back to the woman. She hadn't spoken a word to confirm it, but Robbie already knew who this frail little woman was.

"Thank you," was all he said. The "how" and "why" questions could be dealt with later.

"You're welcome, sweetie," Aggie said. "Everything should be okay now."

"Is my father dead?" Robbie asked.

"No. Not yet."

"He's in the field, isn't he?"

Aggie looked at her feet; neither confirming nor denying, shifting her weight onto the wooden cane.

"Your father can't hurt you anymore."

Robbie thought about that for a moment, his eyes roaming the room and finding his wheelchair again. A dark and vengeful anger began to build within him, then an idea so sweet it brought a smile to his pallid face.

"These flowers you made me," Robbie swept his hand across the pile at his feet. "Can you teach me how to make them? How to *deliver* them?"

Aggie followed the boy's gaze to the wheelchair.

"You want to send your father flowers?" she asked.

"No…something else."

* * *

A middle-aged man lies in a coma.

Fell down the stairs, bumped his head.

Ask his wife, standing by his bedside. She's telling everyone that's what happened.

Don't ask his son, though. No, not him, he's far too busy making giant paper spiders.

Story Notes

Coma and paper cuts. Kind of a strange combination but there's a story behind this unique tale. I have always wanted to get an acceptance into the short story anthology series edited by Thomas Monteleone called BORDERLANDS. To date there have been five of them published and all of them are spectacular. Well, when I heard that Tom was taking submissions for a new volume I was bound and determined to get into the book. Trouble was, Tom is a picky editor and likes his fiction quite literate with unusual, unsettling plots. Standard horror fare need not apply, in other words. So I sat down to come up with something special.

Two days into my quest and the only vision I had come up with was of a young boy sitting all alone in a dirt field. There was nothing around the boy for miles in every direction, which was a strange premise but still no story. I mean, what the heck was this kid doing here? Later that night it finally hit me that the boy was just sitting there because he was lost in the field and didn't know how to find his way home. Okay. Better, but still nothing to work with there, but then my youngest daughter Emily walked into the room and wanted me to help her with some craft she was making. She used to like me to cut out different shapes and things so that she could color them and stick them on the fridge. Being a dad, I wanted to help her out, but being a writer I was multi-tasking, still thinking about story as I was cutting out her crafts. Well, damned if she wasn't asking me to cut out these pictures of flowers and in my head I was thinking...Lost? The boy is lost. He's lost in a field. Lost in a field...of paper flowers! Before I finished snipping out the flowers I was thinking about paper cuts and had the entire plot for my story.

I can't even tell you how many story ideas I've played around with that dealt with a boy in a coma. I have story ideas, novel ideas, and even a couple of movie script ideas. The trouble is I never seem to get around to writing them. I keep telling myself I need to research it more so I get the medical details right but that's probably just a bunch of crap – I'm just good at stalling when I have a topic that really interests me.

Lost In A Field Of Paper Flowers was the one exception I made. The coma angle fit perfectly with what the idea I had come up with so I decided to just let my imagination go wild and to hell with the medical details. It didn't matter how the kid was in a coma or how the old lady could communicate with him, I just created a world where that could happen and ran with it. I never did end up getting into Borderlands but that was because the sixth volume in the series never did make it to print. I still like to kid myself that had the anthology continued on as planned, my story would have been accepted but that's something I'll never know for sure. What I do know, is that this is by far the best short story I've ever written. Not my personal favorite story, and it may not be yours either, but without a doubt it's my most complex and technically solid effort to date.

Well, that about wraps this volume up. I hope you enjoyed these stories.

Gord Rollo was born in St. Andrews, Scotland, but now lives in Ontario, Canada. His short stories and novella-length work have appeared in many professional publications throughout the genre and his novels include: *The Jigsaw Man, Crimson, Strange Magic* and *Valley of the Scarecrow*. His work has been translated into several languages and his titles are currently being adapted for audiobooks.

Besides novels, Gord edited the acclaimed evolutionary horror anthology, *Unnatural Selection: A Collection of Darwinian Nightmares*. He also co-edited *Dreaming of Angels,* a horror/fantasy anthology created to increase awareness of Down's syndrome and raise money for research. He recently completed his newest horror/dark fantasy novel, entitled *The Translators*. He can be reached at his website, **www.gordrollo.com**

More from
Ashbury Creek Media

CROWLEY'S WINDOW
BY *Gord Rollo*

Abby Hawkins was never normal. Born with a birth cowl—a rare birth defect thought to predict psychic abilities—she is haunted by horrible visions. Shortly after her 13th birthday, Abby's parents call in the mysterious Crowley to help their daughter. His interventions rid her of the visions…and her eyes. Now a beautiful young lady, Abby Hawkins works as a blind fortune teller in a traveling Carnival. When she receives a powerful vision—one depicting the abduction of a little girl—she becomes the sole witness to the crime. Only a young police officer believes her bizarre story, and with his help she embarks upon an investigation that will ultimately reunite her with the madman from her past and bring her to the hellish threshold of Crowley's Window.

Valley of the Scarecrow
By *Gord Rollo*

During the great depression, a small backwoods community in Iowa face even more difficult times than most, having to endure the slowly fading sanity of their leader, Reverend Joshua Miller. When it is clear the man has slipped beyond the edge of reason and perhaps signed a deal with the devil, the citizens unite to stop him any way they can, breaking into the church to lash the reverend to his wooden alter cross then boarding up the windows and doors to leave him to fate and God's judgment. The people of Oak Valley then abandoned their town to the cornfields and woods; ending the madness for what they hoped was forever.

Seventy-four years later, the corn and trees have taken back the area and not much is left of the once thriving little community but Joshua Miller's desecrated church still stands, and within its boarded up and sun-baked walls something that used to be a holy man waits for whoever is unfortunate enough to release him from his cross…

The Dark Side of Heaven
By *Gord Rollo*

War can do terrible things to the hearts and minds of even the best of men, but for US Marine Lance Corporal Tyrone Banks the senseless deaths and unnecessary violence in Vietnam have beaten him down and smothered the compassion and good that was once inside of him. Grief stricken and suicidal; the extreme guilt over the awful things he's done pushes the young Marine beyond his breaking point until death feels like his only remaining option.

Rather than eating a bullet, Tyrone volunteers for Tunnel Rat duty hoping to finally find release but instead of his carefully planned honorable death, what the Marine finds down in the dark is a backdoor to Purgatory, a secret entrance into the afterlife where he'll get one last chance to right all the terrible wrongs that constantly haunt him. It won't be easy, though. Nothing worthwhile ever is. If Tyrone thought the things lurking in the jungle of Vietnam were bad, what's waiting for him on the dark side of Heaven is worse.

THE JIGSAW MAN
By *Gord Rollo*

A BROKEN MAN DOWN ON HIS LUCK...

Michael Fox is a homeless man living in a garbage dumpster beneath the Carver Street Bridge in Buffalo, NY. He's bitterly depressed and ready to commit suicide; anything to put an end to his miserable existence.

AN OFFER TOO GOOD TO REFUSE...

When a mysterious billionaire surgeon offers Michael two million dollars for his right arm, he thinks his luck might be about to change. Little does he know that the surgeon has other plans for him. His arm is only the beginning. Bit by bit other pieces of Michael's body are surgically removed; his natural body stripped away and then reassembled using other harvested parts from thirteen 'donor.'

A MODERN DAY FRANKENSTEIN...

Now Fox isn't sure if he's a man or a monster, or whether or not he'd be better off dead. One thing he is sure of though, he's not checking out of this whorl until he finds a way to make the people responsible pay for turning him into the experimental nightmare known as... The Jigsaw Man.

THE FRANCISCAN
BY *James Rollo*

THE JOURNEY

Father Giovanni Moretti, a prominent historian of the Franciscan brotherhood finds his devout routine changed overnight when he accidentally discovers a secret chamber containing an early period Cassock. Stuffed inside the lining of the old robe is a faded hieroglyphic and coded manuscript that will shake his beliefs and remove him from the civilized glory of Rome to the remote and savage frontier of the Wild West.

THE DISCOVERY

With the decoded map entrusted to memory, the Franciscan sets out across the ocean blue on a two-fold mission that will take him on a journey fraught with danger and intrigue. He is not alone however; the sinister figure of Antoine Verdi, swindler and master of disguise stalks his every move.

THE FRONTIER ADVENTURE

It is a time when Pioneers pushed west to the Territory of Arizona and California, lured by gold fever and the prospect of untold riches and land for the taking – Indian land that is. In this historically accurate account, Father Moretti will survive deadly Indian uprisings and the Civil War during his search for the lost Opata mine. After experiencing success and bitter disappointment a surprise turn of events will see the saintly sleuth return to the civilized world where he'll try and turn the tables on the master of disguise himself. Or die trying…

Sons of Thunder
BY *James Rollo*

Killing was nothing new for the Thunders'. They'd lived by the gun since the day they were old enough to pull the trigger...

A SIMPLER TIME WHEN FAMILY MEANT EVERYTHING

Pop Thunder had brought his boys up to know that nothing was free and that anything they wanted would have to be taken, one way or the other and consequences be damned. When that motto eventually gets Pop lynched for cattle rustling his boys' destinies are sealed, their path of revenge chosen for them as they take justice into their own hands to even the score the only way they knew how.

WHEN BLOOD WAS THICKER THAN WATER

Of course, there's always a price to be paid when vigilantes act above the law, and right or wrong, the Sons of Thunder will have to muster their diabolical wits to stay one step ahead of the law, and a trio of dangerous men determined to see them die.

Manufactured by Amazon.ca
Acheson, AB